A L L

M I N E

(A Nicky Lyons FBI Suspense Thriller—Book One)

BLAKE PIERCE

Blake Pierce

Blake Pierce is the USA Today bestselling author of the RILEY PAGE mystery series, which includes seventeen books. Blake Pierce is also the author of the MACKENZIE WHITE mystery series, comprising fourteen books; of the AVERY BLACK mystery series, comprising six books; of the KERI LOCKE mystery series, comprising five books; of the MAKING OF RILEY PAIGE mystery series, comprising six books; of the KATE WISE mystery series, comprising seven books; of the CHLOE FINE psychological suspense mystery, comprising six books; of the JESSE HUNT psychological suspense thriller series, comprising twenty four books; of the AU PAIR psychological suspense thriller series, comprising three books; of the ZOE PRIME mystery series, comprising six books; of the ADELE SHARP mystery series, comprising sixteen books, of the EUROPEAN VOYAGE cozy mystery series, comprising four books; of the new LAURA FROST FBI suspense thriller, comprising nine books (and counting); of the new ELLA DARK FBI suspense thriller, comprising eleven books (and counting); of the A YEAR IN EUROPE cozy mystery series, comprising nine books, of the AVA GOLD mystery series, comprising six books (and counting); of the RACHEL GIFT mystery series, comprising eight books (and counting); of the VALERIE LAW mystery series, comprising nine books (and counting); of the PAIGE KING mystery series, comprising six books (and counting); of the MAY MOORE mystery series, comprising six books (and counting); the CORA SHIELDS mystery series, comprising three books (and counting); and the NICKY LYONS FBI suspense thriller series, comprising three books (and counting).

An avid reader and lifelong fan of the mystery and thriller genres, Blake loves to hear from you, so please feel free to visit www.blakepierceauthor.com to learn more and stay in touch.

ISBN: 978-1-0943-7763-6

BOOKS BY BLAKE PIERCE

NICKY LYONS FBI SUSPENSE THRILLER
ALL MINE (Book #1)
ALL HIS (Book #2)
ALL HE SEES (Book #3)

CORA SHIELDS MYSTERY SERIES
UNDONE (Book #1)
UNWANTED (Book #2)
UNHINGED (Book #3)

MAY MOORE SUSPENSE THRILLER
NEVER RUN (Book #1)
NEVER TELL (Book #2)
NEVER LIVE (Book #3)
NEVER HIDE (Book #4)
NEVER FORGIVE (Book #5)
NEVER AGAIN (Book #6)

PAIGE KING MYSTERY SERIES
THE GIRL HE PINED (Book #1)
THE GIRL HE CHOSE (Book #2)
THE GIRL HE TOOK (Book #3)
THE GIRL HE WISHED (Book #4)
THE GIRL HE CROWNED (Book #5)
THE GIRL HE WATCHED (Book #6)

VALERIE LAW MYSTERY SERIES
NO MERCY (Book #1)
NO PITY (Book #2)
NO FEAR (Book #3)
NO SLEEP (Book #4)
NO QUARTER (Book #5)
NO CHANCE (Book #6)
NO REFUGE (Book #7)
NO GRACE (Book #8)

NO ESCAPE (Book #9)

RACHEL GIFT MYSTERY SERIES
HER LAST WISH (Book #1)
HER LAST CHANCE (Book #2)
HER LAST HOPE (Book #3)
HER LAST FEAR (Book #4)
HER LAST CHOICE (Book #5)
HER LAST BREATH (Book #6)
HER LAST MISTAKE (Book #7)
HER LAST DESIRE (Book #8)

AVA GOLD MYSTERY SERIES
CITY OF PREY (Book #1)
CITY OF FEAR (Book #2)
CITY OF BONES (Book #3)
CITY OF GHOSTS (Book #4)
CITY OF DEATH (Book #5)
CITY OF VICE (Book #6)

A YEAR IN EUROPE
A MURDER IN PARIS (Book #1)
DEATH IN FLORENCE (Book #2)
VENGEANCE IN VIENNA (Book #3)
A FATALITY IN SPAIN (Book #4)

ELLA DARK FBI SUSPENSE THRILLER
GIRL, ALONE (Book #1)
GIRL, TAKEN (Book #2)
GIRL, HUNTED (Book #3)
GIRL, SILENCED (Book #4)
GIRL, VANISHED (Book 5)
GIRL ERASED (Book #6)
GIRL, FORSAKEN (Book #7)
GIRL, TRAPPED (Book #8)
GIRL, EXPENDABLE (Book #9)
GIRL, ESCAPED (Book #10)
GIRL, HIS (Book #11)

LAURA FROST FBI SUSPENSE THRILLER

ALREADY GONE (Book #1)
ALREADY SEEN (Book #2)
ALREADY TRAPPED (Book #3)
ALREADY MISSING (Book #4)
ALREADY DEAD (Book #5)
ALREADY TAKEN (Book #6)
ALREADY CHOSEN (Book #7)
ALREADY LOST (Book #8)
ALREADY HIS (Book #9)

EUROPEAN VOYAGE COZY MYSTERY SERIES
MURDER (AND BAKLAVA) (Book #1)
DEATH (AND APPLE STRUDEL) (Book #2)
CRIME (AND LAGER) (Book #3)
MISFORTUNE (AND GOUDA) (Book #4)
CALAMITY (AND A DANISH) (Book #5)
MAYHEM (AND HERRING) (Book #6)

ADELE SHARP MYSTERY SERIES
LEFT TO DIE (Book #1)
LEFT TO RUN (Book #2)
LEFT TO HIDE (Book #3)
LEFT TO KILL (Book #4)
LEFT TO MURDER (Book #5)
LEFT TO ENVY (Book #6)
LEFT TO LAPSE (Book #7)
LEFT TO VANISH (Book #8)
LEFT TO HUNT (Book #9)
LEFT TO FEAR (Book #10)
LEFT TO PREY (Book #11)
LEFT TO LURE (Book #12)
LEFT TO CRAVE (Book #13)
LEFT TO LOATHE (Book #14)
LEFT TO HARM (Book #15)
LEFT TO RUIN (Book #16)

THE AU PAIR SERIES
ALMOST GONE (Book#1)
ALMOST LOST (Book #2)
ALMOST DEAD (Book #3)

SILENT NEIGHBOR (Book #4)
HOMECOMING (Book #5)
TINTED WINDOWS (Book #6)

KATE WISE MYSTERY SERIES
IF SHE KNEW (Book #1)
IF SHE SAW (Book #2)
IF SHE RAN (Book #3)
IF SHE HID (Book #4)
IF SHE FLED (Book #5)
IF SHE FEARED (Book #6)
IF SHE HEARD (Book #7)

THE MAKING OF RILEY PAIGE SERIES
WATCHING (Book #1)
WAITING (Book #2)
LURING (Book #3)
TAKING (Book #4)
STALKING (Book #5)
KILLING (Book #6)

RILEY PAIGE MYSTERY SERIES
ONCE GONE (Book #1)
ONCE TAKEN (Book #2)
ONCE CRAVED (Book #3)
ONCE LURED (Book #4)
ONCE HUNTED (Book #5)
ONCE PINED (Book #6)
ONCE FORSAKEN (Book #7)
ONCE COLD (Book #8)
ONCE STALKED (Book #9)
ONCE LOST (Book #10)
ONCE BURIED (Book #11)
ONCE BOUND (Book #12)
ONCE TRAPPED (Book #13)
ONCE DORMANT (Book #14)
ONCE SHUNNED (Book #15)
ONCE MISSED (Book #16)
ONCE CHOSEN (Book #17)

MACKENZIE WHITE MYSTERY SERIES
BEFORE HE KILLS (Book #1)
BEFORE HE SEES (Book #2)
BEFORE HE COVETS (Book #3)
BEFORE HE TAKES (Book #4)
BEFORE HE NEEDS (Book #5)
BEFORE HE FEELS (Book #6)
BEFORE HE SINS (Book #7)
BEFORE HE HUNTS (Book #8)
BEFORE HE PREYS (Book #9)
BEFORE HE LONGS (Book #10)
BEFORE HE LAPSES (Book #11)
BEFORE HE ENVIES (Book #12)
BEFORE HE STALKS (Book #13)
BEFORE HE HARMS (Book #14)

AVERY BLACK MYSTERY SERIES
CAUSE TO KILL (Book #1)
CAUSE TO RUN (Book #2)
CAUSE TO HIDE (Book #3)
CAUSE TO FEAR (Book #4)
CAUSE TO SAVE (Book #5)
CAUSE TO DREAD (Book #6)

KERI LOCKE MYSTERY SERIES
A TRACE OF DEATH (Book #1)
A TRACE OF MURDER (Book #2)
A TRACE OF VICE (Book #3)
A TRACE OF CRIME (Book #4)
A TRACE OF HOPE (Book #5)

PROLOGUE

This was it. The moment she'd been waiting for. Nicky Lyons pressed her back to the wall beside the door, her gun out and ready. She held her breath so as not to make a sound. Shutting her eyes, she found her happy place.

Rippling water. A tide slowly rolling in.

Nicky opened her eyes and sucked in a breath.

Game time.

She faced the door and threw her black boot right into the wood, making the lock burst open on this remote cottage off the coast of rural Florida.

The perfect place for this sicko to bring the senator's daughter.

Nicky stepped into the empty cottage with her gun facing forward. As a BAU agent specializing in missing persons, she'd never shied away from getting her hands a little bloody. If it meant saving a missing girl, she would chase a kidnapper to the ends of the earth.

This guy had made a mistake and bought a chocolate bar from a convenience store in the nearby town with his credit card; and Nicky had found out that this cottage had been in his family before but was sold years ago. The fact that it was sold convinced the others back at HQ that the guy likely wouldn't be here.

But then Nicky discovered that the "buyer" of the house seemed to be a completely non-existent person. A guy named Daniel High, who had no birth certificate, no paper trail. He'd bought the place in cash.

Nicky didn't buy it. In fact, she was damn sure that the suspect—Frank Reese—had bought it under the alias "Daniel" just to do whatever sick things he was doing here without getting caught. Nicky was sure "Daniel" was the same person they'd suspected had kidnapped the senator's daughter, Masie, more than a year ago.

He had to be hiding her here.

A place where people could be easily forgotten.

The cottage was dark, and she didn't switch on the lights. Nicky didn't make a sound as she stepped into the living room. She took a deep breath and braced herself against the thought of what she might find. If this guy was the one who stole Masie, keeping her locked up for a year, he was capable of doing anything.

1

Nicky took out her Maglite and switched it on, shining the light around the guest bedroom.

A creak of the floorboard behind her. Nicky's heart stalled.

Someone was right behind her.

Nicky spun. Her eyes met his, shiny as a snake's. He was tall and thin, covered in tattoos. He had one hand behind him, his fingers curled around the handle of a gun.

Frank Reese.

It was really him.

Nicky wasn't about to wait for him to shoot her--she dodged beneath him, just as he fired off a bullet that resounded through the cabin. Nicky got under him and struck his arm upwards, causing his grip to drop the gun. It skidded across the wooden floor. Nicky drew her own gun, ready to shoot--but Frank was fast. He grabbed her wrists and forced them above her head, pointing her gun straight at the ceiling. Nicky fought back with all her strength, but in this moment, she wasn't afraid of dying.

There was only one thing she cared about.

"What have you done with Masie Gregory?" she uttered as she tried to twist her wrists from his grip.

His eyes shone against hers, and a smile curled at his lips before he let out a wicked laugh. And at that moment, Nicky knew, without a doubt, that her hunch was right--this was her guy.

Anger surged through her. She shoved back against him.

"Where is she?" she spat at him, shouting.

He chuckled and pressed her wrists up and forward, increasing the strength of his grip. Nicky's arms shook as she tried to hold back the pain.

"Let her go," she said through gritted teeth.

"Or what?" he taunted.

The words sent a chill down her back. "If you hurt her--"

"You're too late."

Nicky kneed him in the gut, and he let out a wheeze as he dropped her wrists. Nicky quickly regained her balance and moved her gun with lightning speed. She pointed it right at Frank's chest. He froze, but a smirk tugged at his lips that made Nicky's blood burn.

"You're not gonna shoot me," he said. "You're some sort of cop. You can't just kill me. Go ahead and put me in jail, but you won't shoot."

Wanna bet? Nicky wanted to say. But she kept it in. He was right— she couldn't go around murdering suspects if they didn't pose a direct threat to her life or others. But there were some things she could do: "I'll shoot you through the leg if you come any closer," she threatened.

His eyes flicked to the right, where his own gun had landed. Nicky ground her teeth.

"Don't," she warned.

But he didn't listen. He dove right for the gun.

Nicky didn't hesitate.

POP!

Her bullet flew through the air with deadly velocity, hitting the man dead-center in his chest. *No!* She hadn't been going for the kill shot—but she realized, by the way he grabbed at his chest and collapsed to the ground, that she had gone too far.

He went limp on the floor, his eyes glossed over, unseeing.

Nicky swallowed the sick feeling down her throat and crouched next to the body. Her eyes fell onto the man's hands as she turned him over to click on the Maglite. His body was still warm when she touched his neck, but there was no pulse. No breath. She'd killed him.

Nicky's breath came in short bursts. She knew about the people who did all kinds of things to victims--kidnapping, rape, murder--and she'd be lying if she said she felt bad about this one. This guy had been keeping Masie for over a year. Who knows what he had done to her in that time?

But still. Nicky hadn't been planning on taking a life today, and it made her head spin. This was the job. She'd known what she signed up for, and she could never let fear get the best of her.

Now, she had to find Masie.

Going back into the hall, she checked the next room with the Maglite. To her surprise, there was nothing in the room except for a dirty old mattress. But there was a smell in the house. Now that her adrenaline was high, Nicky could feel it.

Something wasn't right.

She hurried down the hall and pushed open the door to the bathroom--her heart sank. The smell was coming from inside the room. She stepped inside and shone the light around the dark room—and her gaze landed on a small, pale body lying on the floor. Nicky took a step closer.

For a moment, her brain didn't register what she was seeing. Her body shook as she reached out to touch the girl--her eyes were open and empty, her face drained of color.

3

Nicky shook her head. No, this wasn't right. It wasn't happening. She'd come all this way. She'd found the guy, and she was not going to let Masie die.

She dropped to her knees and laid a hand on the dead girl's chest. What she didn't notice was the dark, slick substance on her hand until her fingers began to tingle.

Nicky pulled her hand away and saw the blood.

It was still warm to the touch.

The kill had been fresh. He must've done it moments before she'd arrived.

Maybe he even saw her coming up to the building and decided to finish Masie off, right then and there.

Her world crumbled around her.

Masie was dead.

Nicky was too late.

CHAPTER ONE

Nicky entered her dark, quiet apartment, and threw her keys on the console table, not wanting to face what was waiting for her there.

Loneliness. Emptiness.

She would be left with her thoughts, and the memories of what happened. She felt like she'd been hit by a train.

And the only thing that would cure it, or at least numb it, was a stiff glass of whiskey.

She headed straight for the liquor cabinet and took out a bottle of Jack Daniel's, pouring herself a generous glass. Nicky's apartment was dark, save for a lone lamp which cast a dim orange glow through the living room. The light was soft and warm, flickering off the walls.

She'd been living here for the past two years, and she was still surprised each time she stepped into the apartment. The walls were painted a warm honey tone, and the furniture was a step-up from the old discount furniture she'd had in her early twenties. A floor-to-ceiling bookcase was filled with textbooks. But her favorite part was the huge window that looked out to the skyline of Jacksonville, Florida. Nicky took a sip and looked out over the city.

An image of Frank Reese's deranged, snake-like face flashed in her mind.

She wished she could've stopped him, but she'd been too late. But only by a hair. If Nicky had arrived earlier, maybe Masie would still be alive. All the possibilities of things she could have done differently swam through her mind. She could have been faster. She could have been sneakier.

The only thing she was thankful for was that this guy would never hurt anyone again. He was dead. Nicky would be lying if she said he didn't deserve it.

She put the glass to her lips and took a deep breath, feeling the alcohol burn her throat. She'd called in the crime scene and the dead body, and she was damn glad to be out of there. And now, there was nothing she could do anymore. She could never get back what this sicko had taken from the world. A year-long investigation had been nothing but a waste.

Masie would never be back.

Nicky gulped down the rest of the glass. Where the hell was her happy place now?

Twisting the cap off the bottle, she poured another shot and settled on the leather couch, staring at the off TV, but not seeing it--her mind was too busy processing. The booze only burned the pain away; it didn't stop it. She put her glass on the coaster of her glass coffee table.

Nicky's gaze fell onto her cell phone.

She'd left it on silent after she'd called in the murder. Then it was hours spent debriefing at HQ. Now, finally, she was home. But she still felt trapped in that cottage.

Her psychiatrist, Dr. Graham, had told Nicky it was unhealthy to bottle up her emotions; she needed to let them out sometimes. What he really felt like she needed were more friends, more people Nicky could talk to outside of work, but the truth was that Nicky liked to keep her personal life private. It was just easier this way. She socialized with the people she worked with, even went out for drinks with them sometimes, and that was good enough.

Wanting a distraction, she opened her cell and checked her notifications. A text from her mom. A couple of emails.

And one message request on her messenger app. She frowned and opened it up.

It was Matt Haynes.

Nicky hadn't heard from Matt in ages. They grew up in the same small West Virginia town. Thinking about it brought Nicky back to her teen years. The summer heat, watching the sunset as she drank with her friends--Matt included.

They'd all had dreams of escaping.

Nicky dreamed of being an FBI agent. Matt's dream was a little more simple--he wanted to leave home. He wanted to see the world. Nicky wanted to see the world too... but she thought she'd be seeing it while doing her job, not while backpacking across the globe.

That was one thing about Matt--he was always a little over-the-top, but he was never dull. He managed to get into trouble more than anyone Nicky knew, but he was always charming enough to get out of it.

She thought about what Matt had said when she'd last seen him, all those years ago, when they were both eighteen, at high school graduation.

He'd kissed her on the cheek and told her goodbye, but that he'd see her again someday.

Damn, she'd missed him. But she hadn't forgotten him.

6

Nicky opened the message.

Hey, Nicky. When you've got a moment, can we talk? I'm in your area and I'd love to catch up.

Nicky hesitated.

Of course part of her had missed Matt. Missed her old life and the people she used to know.

But her life was unrecognizable now. Now, she hunted kidnappers for a living. Saved girls' lives. Or tried to, anyway. What would she and Matt have to talk about?

Besides, Nicky wasn't in the business of adding more people to her life. It was too complicated. Too much work.

She wrote back: *Sorry, I'm pretty busy with work right now. Great to hear from you, though.*

After she sent the message, Nicky still felt uneasy. She'd always had a soft spot for Matt--and even if she didn't want to admit it, she knew the reason why.

It was the one thing she couldn't escape: she was lonely.

For the past few months, she'd had a fling with another member of the team--a hotshot profiler name Fernando Torres. But it had been more of a physical thing, and that was fine by Nicky. They'd each gotten what they wanted out of it, and it hadn't cost anything, other than the occasional night together--and even then, that was more of a convenience than anything else.

Her old friends were busy living their lives. And Nicky didn't have time for a real relationship.

Matt texted back immediately.

Okay. But I'm staying in town for a few weeks. I'd love to see you.

Nicky shut off her phone. She was a lot of things, but she wasn't a liar. She'd made up her mind. She wasn't going to see Matt. So that was that.

Sighing, Nicky took another swig of her drink and stood up. She was beginning to feel numb. She wandered through her apartment, still holding the drink, with one destination in mind.

Nicky rented a two-bedroom apartment, but the second bedroom wasn't for her.

It was for Rosie.

Nicky entered the room, where she had a massive whiteboard set up.

Clippings of newspapers. Articles. Pictures of her sister.

Everything Nicky knew about Rosie Lyons's kidnapping was in this room. Not only on the whiteboard--but also in Nicky's own memory.

She shut her eyes and pictured the lake. The rippling water...

Maybe it was messed up that she still thought about the lake at that horrible, wretched place as a means to keep her anxiety at bay. The worst days of Nicky's life had happened at that lake house.

But looking out at that water had also been the last time she'd been with Rosie.

In that sense, the nightmare that was the lake house was also a dream.

But Nicky still held onto hope. It had been thirteen years since Rosie was last seen. They never found a body.

She took out her phone and dialed the number of the local police department in Nelly, West Virginia, her hometown. A long way from Florida, where she lived now.

A familiar, gruff female voice sounded on the other end. "Hello?"

Nicky paused. Her voice was thick in her throat. She'd called so many times; the operator, Martha, would recognize her voice. "Hi there, I was calling to ask if any information had come up in a case--"

"It's you again," Martha said. "I'm sorry, sweetie, but there's still nothing new. The case has been cold for years, darling... you know that."

Nicky closed her eyes. This was a call she made every week. She'd called ever since she left her hometown and went into the FBI academy. At this point, it was more of a compulsion than anything. Dr. Graham had mentioned something about that once. He suggested that Nicky making the calls was her way of latching onto hope, because she—and the FBI—had already exhausted every possible lead as to what had happened to Rosie Lyons. The case was colder than the Appalachian Mountains. But Nicky just... needed to call.

"Okay, well... thanks." She hung up.

She headed back into the living room, where she kicked off her shoes and sat on the couch with her cell phone.

Another dead end, as always. But at least it helped keep Rosie's memory alive.

Just as Nicky was about to get up and pour another drink, her phone buzzed. She frowned at the name on the screen. It was late for her boss, Eric Franco, to be calling her, but she picked up.

"Chief, what's going on?" Nicky asked.

"Lyons, you holding up okay?"

Nicky paused. Of course she wasn't. Senator Gregory's daughter was dead, and Nicky had done nothing to stop it. Hell, maybe she even caused it if Frank saw her come up to the cabin. Nicky would never know, because the only two people who truly knew what went on in that cabin were dead.

A thought slithered into Nicky's mind. *Maybe I should just quit. I couldn't save Masie. Maybe I'm not cut out for this anymore...*

"Fine, Chief," she said. "I'm disappointed. But moving on."

"Good. Get some sleep and come in early tomorrow." He paused. "We need to have an important meeting. It's about the case."

Dread filled Nicky's gut.

"What about it?"

There was a long pause on the other end that made Nicky's palms grow sweaty.

"Just make sure you're in," Chief said. "And get some sleep."

CHAPTER TWO

Anxiety grew in Nicky's chest as she stepped into the elevator at work, squinting against the morning light before the doors closed. In only a few short minutes, she'd find out what the chief meant by "important meeting." She didn't feel overly optimistic, and she hadn't been able to shake the thought growing in her head like a malignant tumor. The thought that she'd lost her competency as an agent.

Nicky looked at herself in the mirror of the elevator. She looked pale. The light from the door reflected off Nicky's skin. She could see the highlights in her long dark hair and the gaunt look of her brown eyes. Wearing a black, fitted shirt and black slacks, she looked like she'd been stabbed in the heart and died a number of times through the night.

In reality, she just hadn't slept.

There were several reasons why, but the two biggest were Rosie and the senator's daughter.

She was sure that Masie had suffered before she'd been killed. It was a brutal death. Nicky hadn't been able to shake the images of her lifeless body from her mind.

She wondered how much Rosie had suffered. If Nicky were to believe the police and the media, then she'd know that her sister was dead. But the thing was, Nicky didn't believe them. She didn't want to.

When she entered the office, the room was already buzzing with activity. The thuds of the copier, the ringing of the phone, the soft hum of the air conditioning, the sharp click of a stapler, the sound of a pencil sliding across a desk top, the sound of a ballpoint pen rasping the paper, the clinking of silver serving trays on a desk.

Fernando Torres came up to her, his cheeks slightly red, probably from a hangover. "Hey, Nicky, did you hear about the chief's guest?"

"Enlighten me," Nicky said coldly. Ever since their fling ended, Nicky hadn't been thrilled about Fernando's presence in the office. He didn't exactly handle her ending the fling like a champ.

Fernando raised an eyebrow. "Uh... maybe you should just head into the meeting."

10

Nicky nodded and pushed open the door to a conference room. Fernando was a persistent snoop, so he'd surely been eavesdropping all morning. Nicky couldn't believe she'd ever slept with that guy.

Chief Eric Franco was already sitting at the head of the table, a cup of coffee in his hands. He was in his late fifties, but he was fit, with a shock of thick white hair. He was the head of the BAU unit in Jacksonville and he knew more than anyone in the room.

He caught Nicky's eye and nodded to an empty chair next to him. Early morning sun poured through the windows of the room, and outside, the palm trees and apartment buildings of Jacksonville spread as far as the eye could see. It was a hot, arid day.

Nicky sat down and immediately recognized the other faces at the table.

One was that of Ken Walker, another profiler in the office who'd just been transferred there about a week ago. Ken was in his mid-thirties and was considered the most handsome guy in the office, but he was also stern, distant, and cold. Nicky hadn't exchanged more than a few words with him yet.

Sitting next to him was Kate Pribbenow, one of the FBI's top prosecutors. She was in her forties and had a hell of a career.

Nicky was the youngest one there, only twenty-nine, but she'd worked hard to build up a good reputation at the BAU. Her methods could sometimes bend the rules a little, but she got results.

But there was someone else at the table too.

A beautiful woman in her fifties with ebony skin and matching dark eyes.

This was Senator Amara Gregory.

The senator whose daughter Nicky hadn't been able to save.

Nicky's stomach bottomed out. What was she doing here? She could see the resemblance between Amara and Masie, and it made her insides twist.

"I'm glad you could join us, Agent Lyons," the chief said.

Amara didn't meet Nicky's eyes.

"I'm glad to be here," Nicky said, although she felt uneasy. "What's going on?"

Chief Franco glanced around the room. "First, I want to say that I appreciate each of your being here on such short notice. I know you're all busy, and this is an unusual move to call all of you in at once."

He sounded nervous, which wasn't like Franco at all. Nicky had no idea what was going on here--but she had a bad feeling about it. It was very rare that they'd call their two top profilers into their office, and

11

seeing Kate, the prosecutor, was like seeing some sort of rare species. She was exceptionally busy most of the time but had slotted away time for this meeting. That must mean it was important.

"You're all aware of what happened to Senator Gregory's daughter, Masie," Chief Franco said.

He glanced at Amara, who was sitting at the table with a grim, but stoic expression.

"Agent Lyons here was able to apprehend the killer, but unfortunately, Masie was already lost." A pause. Nicky looked down at the table, clenching her fists, trying to keep it together. "But she's not the only victim."

Nicky's stomach plummeted. She had to say something to Amara-- she had to tell her how sorry she was, but Nicky couldn't find her voice.

Chief Franco said, "Officially, Masie Gregory's case had been labeled as cold, but we didn't give up, and we found the truth. That's all thanks to you, Agent Lyons."

Nicky didn't reply. She knew she didn't deserve any sort of praise. She'd solved the case, sure, but she hadn't been able to save the victim, so none of it truly mattered.

Chief Franco looked at Amara. "Senator Gregory, perhaps you'd like to take it from here."

Nicky forced herself to glance at the senator. Amara's dark eyes were like a laser, focused on Nicky. But then she paced across the room, keeping herself elegant and poised.

"My daughter is not the only girl to have gone missing in this county, and for her case to be labeled cold," Amara said. "We've conjured up a list of ten missing women who have either been declared cold cases or are on their way to becoming declared cold. The women who have gone missing are Meghan Salinger, Amanda Smith, Megan Osterlin, Clara Jones, Paris Connor, Linda Phillips, Delilah Roberts, Brianna Wilcox, and the last two are sisters: London and Paris Knight."

There was a short silence in the room as the team took this in. Nicky didn't know what to make of this—but she had a feeling where it was going.

"That's... a long list," Ken said.

"They all went missing within the last three years," Amara said. "Like my daughter was missing."

The senator walked over to the whiteboard at the front of the room. She picked up a marker and started writing.

She faced the room. "The work isn't over. There are still so many missing girls," Amara said, her voice grave and sad. "Based on recent

12

intelligence we've gathered, we think there could be hope that some of these women are alive."

Nicky's mouth went dry. *We're back on this.*

"I'll keep this simple and get to the point. I want you to form a new task force," Amara said, her voice low and serious. "I want you to go over these cases and try to find clues. Anything that will help us find out what happened to these women."

Nicky's heart hammered in her chest. After all her doubts yesterday—the doubts that still lingered in her mind—she was being given a task far greater than even the Masie Gregory case.

"This is a special mission that I'm organizing with Mr. Franco here," Amara said. "The first woman we are looking into is Meghan Salinger, as we think she's the most likely to be alive--although if our intelligence is correct, she may not have much time left." Amara's eyes hardened on Nicky. "And Agent Lyons, I want you to lead it. I read about your past... and I think you're the perfect person for this job."

Nicky couldn't believe what she was hearing. She'd never been put in charge of an entire mission like this before. And it was so close. So personal.

She thought of Masie's dead body in her arms. She thought of Rosie, still lost out there after all these years.

Nicky's job at the BAU made her a specialist in understanding the motivations and patterns of killers, kidnappers, and other violent criminals, and her speciality was a focus on missing girls. But she typically tackled one girl at a time. Sometimes she could save them. Sometimes she couldn't. It came with the territory.

But to be in charge of ten, high-profile missing women? That was a lot of responsibility. She was already feeling so many doubts about her abilities as an agent. What if she failed them like she'd failed Masie? What if another agent was better suited for the job?

Nicky's stomach twisted. Her hands and face flushed hot.

The room went deadly silent.

"Thank you, Senator Gregory, but..." Nicky swallowed. "I don't think I can accept your offer."

The chief raised his bushy eyebrows and looked at her with his small green eyes. "Excuse me?"

"I... I can't do this," Nicky said. "I can't." Even as she was saying it, Nicky felt her heart squeeze. Maybe she was jumping the gun by saying no, but she wasn't sure how to proceed.

"Agent Lyons..." Chief Franco's voice was sharp, his gaze flicking from Nicky to the senator and back to Nicky. "I'm not sure what you mean. We can't have a team member who isn't fully committed to the cause."

Nicky's stomach turned over and she was almost sick with the realization of what she was doing.

"I'm sorry," she said, her voice barely above a whisper. "But with yesterday's failure, I just... I don't know if I'm the right person for the job right now. After I couldn't save Masie, I..."

Guiltily, she avoided Amara's eyes.

Amara nodded, a grim expression on her face. "Then I understand why you feel that way," she said simply.

"Okay then," Chief Franco said. "But maybe you could take a few days to get your head together, and then we can talk it over, got it?"

"I'll do that," Nicky said quietly.

Amara's eyes fell on Kate and Ken. "Can I count on both of you to be involved?"

Kate nodded, adjusting her fancy suit jacket. "I'll be here to prosecute every kidnapper you find."

"Perfect." Amara looked at Ken. "And you, Agent Walker?"

Ken adjusted his suit jacket over his broad chest. "I can spearhead it if Lyons is out," he said.

A pause in the room. Nicky felt the tension, and Ken's venomous eyes glanced at her. He was still relatively new to the office, and they'd never worked together, but Nicky had heard he was a real by the books guy.

"We will think about that, Agent Walker," Amara said. "Right now, I'd like to give Agent Lyons a few days to think about it."

Nicky felt herself clam up. At this point, she'd rather they just give it to Ken so she could focus on another task. But the least she could do was give it a second thought.

"Thanks," was all she said.

Chief Franco stood. "You're all dismissed."

Everybody stood.

But then Senator Gregory said: "Not you, Agent Lyons. Hold on."

Damn. Nicky had hoped she'd be able to get away. But maybe the senator wanted to try her hand at convincing Nicky again.

Everybody left the room but Senator Gregory and Nicky. Nicky's heart was pounding in her chest. She felt like she was about to face a firing squad.

Nicky remained standing with her hands in fists. "Is there something else, Senator?" she asked politely.

Amara motioned for her to sit down. "Yes. Actually there is. Agent Lyons," Amara said. "After the tragedy that happened to my daughter, I struggled with the most important decision of my life."

Nicky looked at her, curious.

"I had to decide if I could continue doing my job."

Nicky didn't know what to say, so she remained silent.

Amara continued, "But I realized something. Something that no one else seemed to want to tell me."

Nicky watched her, waiting.

"I realized that the only way I could continue doing my job was if I made it personal," Amara said. "If I got involved with the people who disappeared. Agent Lyons," she said, her voice low. "I know it's hard to believe, but I do know what you went through."

Nicky held herself back from turning away. She didn't want to be rude, but the pressure on her was so hot, she felt like she was standing under the sun.

"I know it's hard to be strong," Amara said. "I know it's hard to keep yourself together."

Nicky stared at the floor. She didn't want to talk about this.

"You and I both know what it's like to not have what we wanted."

Nicky felt her lips part. "I'm so sorry about Masie," she said.

"I know," Amara said. "And I'm sorry about your sister."

Amara's eyes softened as she approached Nicky, and she put a warm hand on her shoulder. "I'm not trying to pressure you, Agent Lyons... but please keep these girls in mind. They deserve justice."

Nicky nodded, feeling extremely guilty. "I'll think about it, Senator."

CHAPTER THREE

Late in the evening, Nicky sat in her apartment and sipped a stiff glass of whiskey, scrolling through information on her laptop. She'd told the senator she'd think about her offer more, and she would. And so, she was trying to find out everything she could on the missing girl, Meghan Salinger.

Meghan had been abducted a year ago, right after winning a singing competition. She'd been taken on her way to the studio to record a single.

The media said it was a kidnapping for ransom. But Nicky didn't buy it.

If it was for ransom, why wasn't there a demand?

And why was the girl's body never found?

Nicky read Meghan's news articles, her Wikipedia page, and her social media. She was twenty-four years old, a singer, and a rising star. Nicky clicked through to Meghan's social media account, where she saw a picture of Meghan and a friend named Anne as her last post. All of the comments on the page were wishing for Meghan's safe discovery.

Nicky took another sip of whiskey, feeling her stomach twist with the guilt.

She took out her phone and set it on the table.

The FBI had been working the case from the beginning. But they hadn't even gotten a call from the kidnappers. That was extremely strange in a situation like the one the media had been trying to paint.

Nicky clicked to her FBI database, and she saw that there was little information on the case. Although Senator Gregory had said there was "intelligence," it clearly hadn't been put in the database yet. Nicky couldn't deny her gnaw of curiosity. What type of intelligence was this, and where did it come from?

How did they know if Meghan Salinger was really still alive?

Taking another drink, she felt her head grow hot. Nicky lay back on the couch and pressed her head deep into a decorative pillow, staring up at the stucco ceiling.

Being an FBI agent was in her blood. It had been her calling for years, but sometimes, she felt like it was too much. Nicky was in this to save people, not see them die. Her rational mind knew that losses, deaths, unfortunately came with the territory. But she just didn't want to hunt down another missing girl with the hope she was still alive, only to find her dead in the most brutal way.

It was a lot to bear. Nicky shut her eyes, hoping the darkness would help block out the images of Masie's body.

Before she realized it, she was drifting away. And soon...

Nicky's eyes popped open.

She found herself back at the lake house. But this time, things were different.

Nicky was younger. This was her sixteen-year-old self, wearing a striped tee and jeans. And she was alone with Rosie.

A storm brewed in the distance.

Nicky and her sister were on the beach, watching the water, like they'd done all those years ago. There was a moment of calm, and everything was quiet. Then a wave came, crashing against the sands, and Nicky turned to Rosie. "Do you think the lake remembers?"

Rosie shrugged. "Does it matter?"

Nicky turned toward the lake. "I think it does. I think that's why people come here... they want to remember, even though they know they can't."

Rosie nodded. It was as though she knew what Nicky was thinking.

Then a gust of wind made Rosie's hair whip around her face. "I better get going," she said.

No. Nicky didn't want her to go. She reached out for her.

"Please, stay," Nicky said.

Rosie's eyes softened on hers. Behind her was an expanse of blue.

"I will, on one condition," Rosie said.

"What is it?"

"Nicky..." Rosie's eyes crinkled when she smiled. "Those girls, Nicky. You have to..."

Then the wind picked up, and the rain was coming down. Nicky turned back to the lake and she saw a dozen bodies floating in the water.

And they all had Rosie's face.

Nicky jerked awake. Her breaths were short and heavy. She was drenched in sweat. She sat up on her couch and looked around the living room. Everything was dark and quiet. Nicky closed her eyes, and she could still see the bodies in the lake. And the face of all the missing girls.

17

Her heart was thumping. She couldn't get that image out of her mind.

She needed another drink.

Instead, she sat up and rubbed her eyes, haunted by memories of the past.

It pained her heart to remember what had happened, but as she sat there, alone in the dark, she couldn't stop the onslaught of memories.

Thirteen years ago, Nicky was sixteen years old, and Rosie was fifteen. They had been at the mall in their hometown in West Virginia when they'd noticed a man had been following them for some time. A man they'd never seen before, which was odd considering their town was quite small and close knit.

They left the mall near sunset and walked home beneath an orange sky, feeling the summer air warm on their faces.

The man walked far behind Nicky and Rosie, but the girls kept walking, ignoring him. Rosie glanced over her shoulder, clearly anxious. Nicky was growing apprehensive too, but she tried to just look forward, never looking back.

"That guy is still following us," Rosie whispered as they walked.

"Just don't look at him," Nicky said. "We can't cause a scene. And we'll be home soon."

Nicky was sure they could make it just fine. They grew up on these streets; they knew them. This was a safe town, and maybe the man following them just happened to be on the same path. Nicky's instincts told her otherwise, but she didn't want to scare Rosie. She was the big sister. It was her job to be strong.

They crossed into a park behind the mall and kept walking, even though the man was still behind them.

That was when Nicky realized they were alone.

It was a Sunday, and not many people were out.

Then Nicky heard something.

She turned.

The man had a gun.

His face was obscured by his hoodie, but Nicky could see the bottom half was old, leathery, rugged. They were alone in a park with him. Nicky looked around for any sign of help, but no one was there.

Nicky would never forget the terror she felt as she looked down the barrel of that gun. She and Rosie clung onto each other.

"What do you want?" Nicky asked.

"You're the lucky ones, girls," he said.

"Lucky?" Rosie asked.

18

"You're gonna make it," the man said.

"Make what?" Nicky asked. "Who are you?"

"I'm the man with the power to make all your dreams come true."

Nicky could feel the tightness in her chest--the same tightness she felt now. It was like she was sixteen all over again.

"You girls are coming with me," the man said, a sinister smile tugging at his lips. "You scream, and I shoot."

They'd had no choice but to follow.

Pulling herself from the memory, Nicky gasped for air. She was still on her couch, alone in her apartment. She peered out the window at the skyline and sighed.

The fact that she'd escaped, and Rosie hadn't, was something that had haunted Nicky every single day since. It was a major part of why Nicky had become a BAU agent with a focus on missing girls. Part of her even hoped that one day, she'd find Rosie, somehow, lost among those missing women.

The man who'd taken them was never found either. Nicky had described his van the best she could, but it was a generic make. He had gotten away with what he'd done, and Nicky hated that more than anything.

She went to lie down in her bed and stared at the ceiling, thinking about Masie's body again.

Nicky felt like the ultimate failure for not saving her, and clouded by that failure, she had turned Senator Gregory down. She thought of how compassionate Amara had been earlier. How even in the direct wake of her daughter's death, she was still holding strong, and didn't shed a single tear, not in front of Nicky. She was a strong and admirable woman, and Nicky felt honored that she had chosen her, of all people, to spearhead her team.

Nicky hated that she wasn't able to save Amara's daughter. This loss was a bigger blow than anything she'd experienced in her career so far. But at the same time, Nicky needed to remember why she'd started doing this job in the first place.

Those girls were missing, and they needed help. Like Rosie needed help.

Nicky knew what she had to do next.

CHAPTER FOUR

Meghan never thought she would be wearing a white dress so soon. The gown was long and flowing, like a mermaid's tail on the floor of the cabin. The sheer fabric gleamed like diamond. It was heavy, almost oppressive. The expensive, pure silk scent of the gown had no smell, like a statue of a bride.

"You look so radiant," he told her, wearing a smile. His smile was yellow, contrasting against the white shirt he had beneath his crisp suit jacket and tie.

Meghan tried not to tremble.

He hated when she showed fear.

"I simply can't wait for our big day," he told her. "I know a husband is not supposed to see his wife in her wedding dress beforehand, but I just couldn't resist..." His brown eyes slithered up her. "You are just so perfect."

Meghan felt tears mace her eyes. If he didn't have a gun, she would scream, run, try to escape. But she knew she couldn't. She'd tried before, and that was how she got the bruise that still swelled up her left eye. She didn't want to try again. Because she knew he would hurt her much worse next time.

"Oh, don't cry, my dearest. You'd better not be a runaway bride..." He chuckled to himself, making her stomach curl.

Meghan turned away from him, and he sighed.

Then he took her in his arms, and said, "I'm sorry. I just get so lonely."

"I'm tired," she lied.

He kissed her on the neck and licked her ear and whispered, "Let me show you how lonely I am."

He brought his lips to her ear, kissing her, and she shuddered.

His breath was foul. Everything reeked, everything felt wrong.

When he pulled away, she let out a breath of relief. Maybe he was done with her for today.

"I bought you a present," he said, grinning.

Meghan hated every second of this. The fear she felt was like nothing she'd ever experienced, and this entire thing had been a nightmare. But she also knew by now that she had to play along. If she didn't, he would get angry. "You didn't have to..."

He was holding a box. It was black. She reached out.

"Go on," he said, pulling her hand closer.

She opened the box.

It was a silver necklace, and it looked old and dated. The chain was tarnished, but the pendant was still fine and shiny. On the pendant was a charm, a silver heart.

"You love it, don't you?" he said.

Meghan trembled and nodded. She was terrified to do anything else.

He kissed her again, and she closed her eyes, trying to think of something to keep him from hurting her.

The necklace was a cheap piece of junk.

She should have known. He would find so many reasons to lie to her about why he was doing this, but she didn't care anymore.

Her mind was full of nightmarish images of him chasing after her, of him snatching her from that parking lot all those nights ago. How long had it been now? Days? Months? Meghan had lost count.

"Why don't you wear it with your dress?" he said.

Meghan didn't reply, just continued to tremble.

"Oh, my dear, you're far too quiet." He took the necklace and moved behind her, and she stiffened as the cold chain appeared around her neck. "You better find your voice, my love."

He adjusted the chain on her chest.

"If you don't read me the perfect vows..."

He clicked the clasp shut, then moved his lips to her ear. Meghan's heart stuttered. Fear coagulated in her veins. She held her breath as he said:

"Then it will be the death of you."

CHAPTER FIVE

Nicky entered Chief Franco's office first thing in the morning, and he looked up at her from beneath his glasses. The chief's office smelled like old coffee and stale cigarettes and the paper waiting to be recycled, and light poured in through the windows. "Agent Lyons, you're here early."

It was true. Mostly because she hadn't slept. Nicky left her apartment an hour earlier than she usually would, but this couldn't wait. She faced the chief firmly.

"Chief, I changed my mind. I'd like to accept Senator Gregory's proposal."

The chief didn't look surprised. He nodded, tapping his fingers on his desk, thinking about what Nicky had said. Then he spoke. "This is a high-profile case, Agent Lyons. You're in charge of a special task force, and you can expect heaps of media pressure, with Senator Gregory's name attached to it. If anything goes wrong..."

Nicky knew the risks. She knew this was a big deal.

But it wasn't just about the senator. It was about all the girls that were missing out there.

When the chief finished talking, Nicky nodded.

"I understand," she said. "I'm ready to take on the task, even with the risks."

"Good," the chief said. "Because I wouldn't have given this to you otherwise." A smile tugged at his lips. "But I knew you'd change your mind. The senator will be ecstatic." Franco stood up, his chair skidding against the floor as he did. Behind him, the city stretched endlessly into the morning sky.

Nicky felt good about this. Optimistic.

If she didn't want any more dead girls on her hands, then, well, she would just have to act faster and get the job done better. She'd have to work harder. She'd have to save them first.

"Come on," the chief said. "Let's go meet the rest of your team."

Franco led Nicky through the bustling office, their steps echoing off the walls. People hurried back and forth, carrying files and talking on their phones. They passed the reception desk and turned a corner, finally coming to a briefing room. The walls were a deep, rich red. The

22

floor was polished wood. The windows were large and let in light and air. A large table with chairs was in the center of the room. A map of the city was taped to one of the walls.

Inside, Agent Ken Walker was sitting down, reading over some paperwork. Nicky had a feeling working with him could create some friction, but at the same time, she was looking forward to seeing his skills.

The other person was new. A short, spindly girl with brown hair and big doe eyes stood at attention as soon as the chief and Nicky walked in.

She was one of those girls that would look adorable if she wasn't so fierce looking. Her features were delicate, but the sharpness of her eyes hinted at a toughness that lay just beneath the surface. She was short enough that she'd be beneath most of the other girls in the office, but her body was lithe and graceful. She looked like she could fight and win, and that was a good thing.

"Agent Lyons," Chief Franco said, "This is Agent Grace Taylor. She's an up-and-comer in our office, a real savvy tech. She's been doing very well, and she'll be working closely with you."

Nicky didn't know what to think. She'd seen her type before. A petite girl, an attractive girl, a girl that wasn't being taken seriously, not by other agents. But sometimes, those girls were the ones with the fiercest souls. Nicky wasn't about to pass judgement on Grace—she just wanted to see what the girl could do. She looked determined to prove herself.

"Agent Lyons," Grace said, walking forward. She shook Nicky's hand. "It's nice to meet you. I've heard a lot."

"Nice to meet you too," Nicky said.

"And you already know Agent Walker," the chief said, nodding at Ken. Ken stood up and stiffly nodded.

"Lyons. You changed your mind," he droned out. Nicky wondered if he was slightly bitter she'd been chosen instead of him.

"I'm looking forward to working with you, Walker," Nicky said.

"Likewise," Ken muttered as he sat back down.

"Agent Lyons, what are your initial thoughts on how we should proceed?" the chief asked.

Nicky felt all eyes on her, and the pressure that she was the leader of this suddenly became real. But she needed to prove she could handle this, so she kept her back straight, her posture strong.

"Well, Chief, first, I need to know exactly who we're dealing with here. Senator Gregory mentioned the first victim we're to focus on is

Meghan Salinger. We need to know everything we can about her--who she was, when she went missing. Everything."

The chief flicked off the lights and pulled out an overhead projector. Nicky sat down next to Grace at the table, ignoring the sour look she received from Ken.

The chief turned on the projector, filling the dark room with a pale white light. He turned on the computer connected to it. Then, he loaded up a picture of Meghan.

"This is Meghan Salinger, twenty-four," the chief said. "She vanished a year ago on her way to a studio in Southern Florida to record her first single. A rising music star, she was growing quite the impressive social media following before she was taken. We theorized she'd been kidnapped for a ransom, but we never heard from the kidnappers."

"So how the hell do we know she's still alive?" Ken asked. He leaned back in his chair, arms crossed over his broad chest.

"Good question," Nicky cut in. "I'm wondering the same thing, Chief. Senator Gregory said there was intelligence reported on Meghan Salinger, and I need to know exactly what that intelligence was, where it came from, and how credible it is."

"Lyons, I agree with you." The chief used a remote to flick to another image on the projector screen. This one was a mugshot of a sallow-faced man in his late fifties or early sixties. His eyes were dull, and they seemed to stare straight into Nicky's soul.

"This is Bernard Brown," the chief said. "A convicted serial killer with a long history with the law. Brown is our intelligence in this case."

Nicky, Ken, and Grace all exchanged confused looks. Nicky sensed they were all thinking the same thing--what did a convicted serial killer have to do with this? He was surely already in jail when the girls went missing.

"I can see your confusion," the chief said. "Let me explain. Brown shared a cell with another convicted felon--a murderer named John Wentz. Brown testified that Wentz claimed he had a friend on the outside who had made a bet with him that he could make a girl vanish without a trace, without actually killing her. Meghan Salinger went missing around the same time Brown claims Wentz's friend made such a statement, and he was in the same area of Southern Florida, so the timeline matches up."

Nicky thought on it. It was a convoluted trail--but it could lead somewhere. "So we should talk to Wentz," Nicky said, "not Brown."

The chief held up a hand. "One problem with that, Lyons. Wentz is dead. Brown killed him in his cell."

Silence spread throughout the room. Of course--with Nicky's luck, Wentz being alive would be too convenient.

"So the only lead we have is Brown," Nicky said. "And it's hearsay from a clearly deranged murderer."

"That's right," the chief said.

"But Brown is the only convicted killer we have with a possible connection to this case. We don't want to overlook a lead that could save a lot of lives, especially if it's this one."

"But what can we do with it?" Grace said, her doe eyes wide. "How do we even use this lead? Can't we just confront Brown with the information on Meghan Salinger and ask him to help?"

Ken let out a grunt. "I doubt it'd work that easily—the guy is a felon. He won't be eager to help us."

"I didn't say it would be easy," Grace said, her slender fingers drumming on the table. "But we have to try."

"You're right," Nicky said. "We have to try, even if there's a slim chance this could lead us to find what happened to Meghan."

"Then what do we do?" Grace turned to face Nicky, hope in her eyes.

Nicky nodded. She knew this case was going to be tough. But it could be done. She could do this.

"We'll proceed with caution," she said.

"You're in charge, Agent Lyons," the chief said. "Whatever you need, you'll get."

Nicky nodded. Now that most of her nerves had cleared, she could process how great this opportunity was for her career. This was her chance to excel. Nicky wasn't the kid at the office anymore; she was twenty-nine, going on thirty in a few months, and she was eager to show everyone what she could do when given the reins.

"Good luck, agents." The chief flicked off the projector, leaving the room in darkness. Moments later, the light flicked on. The chief looked down at them. "I'm leaving this all in your capable hands. Remember, Agent Lyons is in charge." The chief looked at Ken when he said that. "Follow her orders."

With that, Franco left the room. Silence. Nicky glanced around the table awkwardly. Ken looked unimpressed. But Grace was looking to Nicky like a hopeful puppy.

"Well," Nicky began, clearing her throat. She needed a game plan for them, and she needed it now. This was her first time in charge of a team--but she didn't want it to be her last.

"I'm sure we can all agree that the prison lead is flimsy," Nicky said. She swallowed her nerves. "But it's the best thing we've got."

Nicky thought over the plan. No matter what, as the only other field agent, Nicky was going to end up working closely with Ken. Grace was a tech, so she was most useful staying here where she could have all the resources of the BAU at her disposal. The computers in the BAU's bullpen were state of the art. They had access to the latest forensic software and databases. They had access to the latest intelligence reports. Nicky was grateful for their help, but she knew that she couldn't rely on them. She had to be self-sufficient. That was why she was the field agent. She was the one who had to be able to think on her feet and make quick decisions.

"Okay, game plan," Nicky said. "Grace, you stay here at HQ and learn as much as you can about the victim, and this John Wentz guy while you're at it."

"You're the boss," Grace said.

"You go get set up," Nicky said, noting the time.

Grace left, leaving her and Ken alone in the room. Nicky felt her palms grow sweaty as she faced him. He eyed her up, and she wasn't sure what he was thinking. But then he said:

"You've never led a team before, have you?"

A lump formed in Nicky's throat, but she nodded. "No, Agent Walker, I haven't."

He nodded. "Well, I have. If you need any tips…"

She couldn't help but glower at his tone.

"Or," Ken said, "I could just take over if you're not up for it."

Nicky crossed her arms. She didn't know Ken well, since he was still a new transfer to the office, but that meant he didn't know her well either. She wasn't the type to take patronization—from a man, no less. It was hard enough being a woman in a field like this, and she didn't get as far as she did by having no voice.

"I appreciate the offer, Agent Walker," Nicky said, "but make no mistake: I've been put in charge of this team, which means you follow my lead." She eyed him up, but his blue eyes didn't leave hers. "I might have less field experience than you, but I was chosen for a reason. Don't forget that."

They locked eyes for a long, tense moment, before Ken shrugged and turned away, hands in the pockets of his pants. "Like Grace said, you're the boss. So, what do we do next?"

Nicky couldn't deny the idea of working closely with Ken after that was unappealing. But she couldn't let that ruin this. She had to get this right. This was her first chance to lead, and she was going to seize it with both hands.

She took a seat at the table. She needed to follow this case, to prevent more girls from disappearing.

She looked at the projector screen, where the mugshot of Bernard Brown stared at her.

"We're going to find this girl, and we're going to make sure she's safe. Until then, we have to go over the details of Bernard Brown," Nicky said. "We need to know all the information we can get. Because we need to be ready to go if we get a lead." She turned to Ken. "I want to know everything about this Brown guy."

"I'm still not sure about this," Ken said. "But whatever you think is best, let's do it."

"Good." Nicky's eyes hardened on his. "In that case, you and I need to catch a flight."

CHAPTER SIX

Nicky felt a rush of adrenaline as the plane swooped to a steady descent. She had the window seat, with a full view of Southern Florida beyond; through the clouds, grasslands emerged, followed by a span of forest. As the plane continued to fly on a steady downward trend, Nicky found herself staring down at the sun-bleached sand of the beach.

Ken was beside her, and he'd been quiet the whole flight as he read a book--one Nicky noted was on human psychology. Nicky didn't mind the silence; she had nothing to say to Ken, anyway, and it was obvious he didn't like her, or respect her as his boss. But he would just have to get used to it, because this case wasn't about Ken. It wasn't even about Nicky. It was about Meghan Salinger.

Still, Nicky wanted to clear the air with him before they were officially working together. She needed to know that she could rely on him.

"Ken," she said. He peered over the edge of his book, his eyes narrowing. So he really didn't like her, did he? Nicky felt her nerves return. "I just wanted to say I appreciate you helping out on this case. I can tell you're not my biggest fan, and that's fine. But we need to work together, so let's make sure we're on the same page. Okay?"

Ken's eyes narrowed further. He wasn't impressed. But he answered her question, anyway. "I never said I didn't 'like' you, Agent Lyons," Ken said. "But I think you're in over your head. You're young, and I just think you lack the experience to lead a team like this. I've led dozens in my career, so I apologize if I feel like they gave the wrong person the job."

Nicky couldn't fight the offense that rose in her. "You might be older than me, Agent Walker, but you know I have a solid track record. I'm more than fit to lead this case. The senator and the chief thought so."

Ken grunted and looked away. "I hope they're right, for those girls' sakes."

Nicky's chest tightened. He'd struck a chord. Of course, her biggest fear on this case was letting those girls down, but she couldn't think like that. Not anymore.

"We'll save them," Nicky said. She looked at Ken's profile. He was clean-shaven with a broad jawline and rough, but handsome features. Black hair and light blue eyes, inky lashes. "But Ken," she said, "I need to know you're with me on this."

He met her eyes. Then, a sigh. "I'm with you. We're gonna get this done. But don't be surprised to hear me speak my mind if I think you're off-base."

"Fair enough," Nicky said. She turned back to look out of the window. The plane was almost on the ground now. It was time to leave the comfort of the plane and get to work.

Nicky was rooted to her seat. The beach they'd flown over was now just twenty feet below. Nicky gazed out of the window at the expanse of golden sand, and the ocean beyond. Sunlight glittered on the surface of the sea. After a few moments, the tires of the plane hit the tarmac with a soft thud.

Nicky and Ken made their way through the busy airport. People talked loudly on cell phones while they walked, luggage hit the floor as some shoved past her. Nicky saw a young girl with a broken arm being carried by her aunt. The girl was sobbing--whether from the pain or the fear, Nicky wasn't sure. Airports had always made her anxious. It was so busy, so crowded, and she was surrounded by so many different people. It all added to the buzzing inside her mind.

Still, she was determined not to let the anxiety show, so she walked on, following Ken to the exit.

A warm breeze blew through Nicky's hair as they left the airport, heading out onto the street. The sun beat down. The air smelled of salt water, and of flowers. The sun was hot on Nicky's skin, but it felt pleasant, like this was the place to be. Growing up in West Virginia, which was much darker and cooler than Florida, made Nicky grateful for every day she got to step out and get a natural tan.

"Come on," Nicky said. "Let's get our rental car and get to the prison. We've got a long drive ahead of us."

"How far is it?" Ken asked.

"It's about two hours away," Nicky said. "It's a lot of driving." She hoped Ken wouldn't fight her for the wheel.

Being stuck in a vehicle for extended periods of time always reminded her of what happened all those years ago, right before Nicky and Rosie were abducted. They were driven in a van that smelled of mildew and old coffee to the edge of their town. Then the man took them deep into the woods through a narrow trail. He drove them down to the lake, which had been forgotten by the rest of the world.

The lake...

Nicky couldn't think about that here. She shook the memories from her mind and focused on Ken.

"I can drive if you want to rest," he said.

"I'm fine," Nicky said. She needed to keep her eyes on the road. While it was true that being stuck in a vehicle made her anxious, nothing made her more anxious than being the passenger. That was what would really remind her of what happened, and Nicky couldn't stomach that. She needed to be behind the wheel, because she needed to keep control. "Besides, it'll give me a chance to learn more about you," she said. "You'll just be sitting there enjoying the scenery, so you can tell me all about yourself."

"What's to learn?" Ken said, his eyes hard. "I'm just another guy. Not much to see here."

Nicky jutted her lip, actually having a moment with Ken. She remembered the book he was reading on the way up and dished up something faux-insightful: "Everyone thinks they're just like every other person. That they're normal. But they're not. Everyone has something that makes them unique. Maybe you'd be better at helping me out if you were a little more self-aware."

"Where'd you get that one, a horoscope magazine?" Ken shot back.

Nicky nearly laughed. "Very original."

Once they located their rental car, Nicky got behind the wheel. Ken took the passenger seat, and they drove out of the airport, heading down the wide road leading to the highway. Tropical trees fanned over the road, and the sun beat down on them.

Nicky had the radio turned on low, and both agents were quiet. She tried not to let her eyes stray to Ken, but she was being serious before about learning about him. Nicky didn't have friends outside of work, but the truth was that somewhere inside of her, she was still a social butterfly, remnants of who she used to be before she left West Virginia. Maybe it was the trauma of what happened, but she had a much easier time talking to people at work outside of it, because having people actually in her personal life made her feel too vulnerable. But at work, things felt different.

Ken was quiet, though, and Nicky figured a guy like him would be hard to get to know.

"This is some place," she said finally, gazing out at the Florida landscape surrounding the highway. Palm trees reached into the cerulean sky. With the window down, the air was humid, the constant wind carrying smells of the sea and rich, tropical earth.

"Yeah, it's not bad," Ken agreed.

Taking the moment to learn more about him, Nicky asked, "Where are you from, Agent Walker? We've been in the same office for at least a month, but I barely know anything about you."

Ken glanced at her, one eyebrow raised. "You know everything you need to know about me, Agent Lyons," he said.

"I know you were transferred from Portland, but that's about it," Nicky said.

"What about *you?*" Ken asked, deflecting. Nicky sighed. Of course he'd turn this around on her, but Nicky was more comfortable being open about her past.

"I knew I wanted to join the FBI in high school," she said, "so I went into the academy as soon as I moved away from West Virginia. I became the youngest field agent in my class."

"Impressive," Ken muttered. "West Virginia. That's pretty different from Florida. Why the switch?"

Nicky looked out at the sunny scenery that surrounded them. "Things are just... brighter here," she said.

From then, they traveled on in silence. Nicky's grip was tight on the wheel. Ken sat staring out of the window, his arms crossed, still a stone wall. But if he didn't want to chat, it made no difference—she wasn't on this case to become best friends with Ken Walker. She was on it to save girls' lives. She just hoped she'd be able to keep it together—and keep Ken on her side as the leader of this team.

***

The prison finally came into view. Beyond the fence, the imposing building rose up out of the ground like an enemy bunker. The prison was made of white concrete, three stories high and solid. The razor wire atop the fence was electric, the current strong enough to light up the skies if touched. Guards patrolled the fence, their rifles at the ready, just in case.

Nicky's chest tightened as she parked the car. This Bernard Brown guy--his mugshot had looked bone-chilling, and Nicky wasn't looking forward to meeting him.

On the flight up, she'd been reviewing his file, getting to know his long history of crimes. He was an active serial killer thirty years ago. The file said there were over a dozen victims. Now, he was a man serving a life sentence in a maximum-security prison.

31

The world was a better place without him, Nicky reflected. But his murderous ways didn't stop in prison. He'd killed a cellmate once before, fifteen years ago, and was put in isolation for eight years before finally being let back out. Obviously, he ended up killing a cellmate again, so he had been put back in isolation. Nicky couldn't help but think it was a gross lapse in judgement for them to ever think he could be trusted with a cellmate again, but after all those years, they must have made the call.

Ken and Nicky were met at the gate by a guard. He took their weapons and then escorted them inside. Inside the main building, it was bright and clean, but that didn't make Nicky feel any better. There were still bars everywhere, and the guards were watching their every move. Prisons weren't her favorite place in the world, and often, when she was in them, she couldn't help but think about the man who'd taken her and Rosie all those years ago, and how this was where he belonged. But he was still out there, free. It all made Nicky's blood burn.

Nicky glanced at Ken, still silent. "Hope you like being in a maximum-security prison," Nicky said to Ken, trying to break the ice.

"It's just business as usual," he muttered, although he looked as disturbed by their surroundings as she did.

They were led down a corridor, and then left into a small room. A guard took their IDs and then left them alone.

"So, how are we doing this?" Ken asked. "Are you gonna be in charge of the interrogation?"

"It's not an interrogation, per se," she said. "At least, we don't want it to feel like one. We just want to ask him some questions, that's all."

"Right," Ken said.

The guard returned and escorted them into another room that was even smaller, containing just a table and a few chairs. In one of the chairs sat a man who, up until that moment, Nicky had only seen in his mugshot.

Bernard Brown.

He was a large man, in his late sixties, with white hair and a friendly smile. His blue eyes were cold, though. Bernard was dressed in prison scrubs, his hands handcuffed behind his back, and he had a crazed, yet amused look on his face.

"You must be Agent Lyons," Bernard said with a smile. His voice was friendly, too. "I would love to shake your hand, but..."

"No pleasantries necessary," Nicky muttered, ignoring the disturbing sensation she felt, looking into the eyes of this killer.

32

Ken was quiet, but Bernard was only looking at Nicky. She felt uncomfortable under his stare. According to his file, most of Brown's victims had been men. But maybe he hadn't seen a woman in a long time, and that was why he couldn't stop staring at Nicky.

Either way, it made her skin crawl.

"So," Bernard said, "how can I help you fine folks?"

Nicky cleared her throat and tried to look strong as she met his eyes. "You were John Wentz's cellmate," Nicky said.

A flicker of emotion crossed Bernard's face. Maybe even joy, likely at the memory of killing Wentz. "I was."

"We understand that Wentz confided in you about a friend," Nicky said. "A friend he claimed abducted a girl."

"Wentz was a liar," he said. "He liked to talk a lot, but he always lied. He was a very bad person."

"Just tell us the truth, Brown," Ken said. "We're not here to play games."

The old man smiled at Nicky. "You're a very beautiful young woman, Agent Lyons," he said. "It's too bad you chose such a... *masculine* career path."

Nicky's eyes narrowed. "I'm here to ask you about John Wentz," she said. "Not about my looks."

"I'm only saying the truth," Bernard said. "I see you're a woman. I'm only saying your beauty is a truth I see. You would be much better suited for something that complements such beauty, but then again, if that were the case, I wouldn't be blessed by your image on this fine day."

Nicky wanted to slap him. She wanted to get up and leave, but she had to be professional. She had to be the agent that the FBI needed her to be, so she ignored his dehumanizing comments and continued, "Are you suggesting that Wentz lied about what he said about his friend?"

"Oh, no, that might have been a truth," Bernard said. "But how can we really know?"

"Did he ever mention the name of that friend?" Nicky asked.

Bernard went quiet. "Hmm. A name, you say. Wouldn't that be valuable information? If only I had it."

"Listen, shitbag," Ken said. Still, not once, had Bernard looked away from Nicky, not even as Ken spoke. "If you give us the information we need, you might get rewarded with a book to read inside your isolation cell."

33

"Young man," Bernard said, eyes still on Nicky, "if one cannot sit alone with their thoughts and be content, then they are not complete individuals. Wouldn't you agree, Agent Lyons?"

Nicky didn't reply, but she felt like bugs were crawling all over her skin. Brown's stare was unnerving. Nicky had met dozens of psychopaths and creeps alike in her career, but something about this one felt... different. She couldn't place what it was.

"I will tell you one thing, and one thing alone," Bernard said, eyes buggy, but firm. "All roads lead to home, Agent Lyons. All roads lead to home."

Ken shoved away from the table. "This is a waste of time."

Nicky stood, too, but she held Bernard's eye contact and considered his words. *All roads lead to home.*

They left the interrogation room as Bernard shouted the phrase over and over again, cackling loudly, "All roads lead to home!"

Once back in the hallway, Ken slammed the door behind them and faced Nicky, but Nicky was still back in that room, replaying Brown's words the same way he'd yelled them.

"That was useless," Ken said. "That guy was just trying to toy with us."

Nicky couldn't deny that he was playing a game back there. At the same time, maybe Brown was implying something with his words. If it was a game, maybe that was the hint on how to "win." Maybe "home" could mean Meghan Salinger's home?

It wasn't that helpful, but Nicky decided that maybe the best route was to talk to the victim's family.

CHAPTER SEVEN

Nicky pulled the car up to a diner off the highway, near a small town about an hour away from Hollywood (the Florida one, of course). The diner was squat and white with a red stripe on the side and a sign above the door that read "Hogan's". The parking lot was fairly full. Being so close to Hollywood, Nicky could tell this place got a lot of business. It wasn't a big or impressive building, but it did have that classic 1950s diner appeal.

Meghan Salinger's parents owned this diner; it had been in the family for two generations. Meghan had planned to break out of the family mold and go after a singing career.

Nicky and Ken got out of the car and went inside the diner. The door dinged as they entered. The diner was sit-down style, with stools at the counter and booths along the walls. There was an old fashioned jukebox in one corner, and a soft jazzy tune was playing from it. The diner smelled of bacon, hash browns, and hot coffee. Various people sat around, and waitresses zipped back and forth between tables. The light from the neon sign above the door shone in through the windows, casting a warm glow over the customers and the kitchen.

Behind the counter was a woman with striking features. Her face was round and her skin was smooth. She had long, curly hair that was pulled back into a bun and she wore a white apron over a red blouse. Her eyes were a deep green and they shone with intelligence and warmth. Nicky immediately recognized her from Meghan's file. This was her mother, Linda Salinger.

"Mrs. Salinger?" Nicky asked.

She looked up. Nicky and Ken both held up their badges, and Linda went pale.

"We're with the FBI," Nicky said. "We were hoping to ask you a few questions about your daughter."

Linda's face twisted. "What? Did you find something out about Meghan?"

"I'm afraid not, ma'am," Nicky said. "But Meghan's case has been officially handed over to the FBI, and we were hoping to learn as much as we can from you. Is there somewhere more private we can talk?"

Linda was flustered, but she said, "The kitchen. Follow me."

They followed her through the diner to the back, where a door led to the kitchen. They passed through a small hallway and then entered the kitchen. As she led them back, the smell was even stronger: bacon, eggs, and fresh bread. The kitchen was a small one, with a narrow counter along the wall and stools in front of it.

There, they sat down at a small table with Linda.

"I'm sorry we have to do this," Nicky said. "This must be difficult for you."

"I thought I was done with this," Linda said, lowering her head. "I thought this was over. I thought I could put it behind me. I thought my daughter couldn't be found."

"I know this is hard," Nicky said. "But we can't go forward with our investigation without your help. We do believe there's a chance your daughter could be found alive."

Suddenly, a man burst into the room. Nicky recognized him as Meghan's father, Terry Salinger. He had a wild look in his eyes, and he was panting heavily. Terry looked like he'd lost his mind. He looked at the three of them, his eyes going from person to person, then back to Nicky. "What the hell is going on?" he asked, his voice sounding out-of-breath. "We already talked to everyone we could about our daughter. If you're here to traumatize my wife more, I won't have it!"

Nicky held her hands up. "We're not here to cause you more harm, sir. We just have questions."

"Who the hell are you people?" Terry demanded.

Nicky introduced herself and Ken again. "We're part of a special task force--"

"That only exists to make families suffer!" Terry roared. He was a big man, with a barrel chest. He had a thick, dark mustache and a shaved head. "You're probably here to tell me you're doing nothing! That you screwed up, and now you want to pump my wife for information when our daughter is gone!"

"Mr. Salinger--"

"She's dead, damn it! She's gone, and there's nothing more we can do!" He picked up a plate from the rack and went to throw it. Nicky braced herself--but Terry caught himself and stopped, taking a deep breath. He put the plate down. The tension in the air was so thick it could be cut in two.

"What makes you so sure Meghan is dead?" Nicky cautiously asked.

"Because," he said, "the police had months to figure out what happened when I told them who it was all along. It was her damn ex-

36

boyfriend. Everyone knew it, but those incompetent cops wouldn't listen. They should've arrested the asshole when they had the chance."

Nicky exchanged a look with Ken, who wore a confused, but stern expression.

"And what's this guy's name?" Ken asked.

"Darren McMillan," Terry said. "That guy is a real piece of work."

Nicky glanced at Linda for confirmation. She held herself, looking sad, but nodded. "I also believe Darren wanted to hurt Meghan. He was very possessive, and when she broke it off with him, we all feared violence."

"And then she disappeared," Nicky said. "How long after they broke up?"

"About two months," Linda said.

"He'd been stalking her at work. She'd come home upset and would stay holed up in her bedroom for days. I asked her to come home, but she wouldn't. She'd just stay in there, crying. I think she was afraid of what Darren might do."

"She got her locks changed, but he broke them," Terry said. "One day, I drove by and I saw him parked outside her work. He saw me, too. I went inside and told the cops, but when I went outside again, he was gone. He's slick."

"There's got to be something you can do," Linda said, tears in her eyes. "It's been months, but she's still missing. There's got to be something--"

"We're doing everything we can to find your daughter," Nicky said. "We're slowly unraveling this case. We have some leads, and we're following them wherever they go."

Nicky and Ken stood up. "Thanks for the info," Ken said. "We'll look more into Darren."

"I need more than that," Terry seethed. "I need you to arrest him."

"We'll do what we can," Nicky told him. "I promise you that much."

She took another look at Meghan's parents, who were so obviously broken up over their missing daughter. "We want to find her just as much as you do."

Nicky and Ken left them to their grief.

***

Nicky's heart was racing as she called Grace right away. The sound of the phone ringing filled the car and Grace's voice came through the speakers immediately. It was warm, calming, and reassuring.

"Agent Lyons! Have a task for me?" Grace asked through the phone.

"I do," Nicky said. "I need you to dig up some intel on a guy named Darren McMillan, from a small town near Hollywood called Frankstown."

"You got it, babe," she said. "Give me a sec."

Nicky heard typing on the other end of the line. She adjusted herself in the driver's seat. Ken was on the passenger side, silently looking at the world outside. Through the windshield of the car, the sun was sinking in the sky, turning the sky yellow in the late-afternoon.

Shortly, Grace came back with: "Wow, this guy is a real piece of work, that's for sure. On paper, he's only been dinged for a few minor drug charges... but I did some deeper digging and apparently he's been linked to human trafficking, but he was too good at covering his tracks for it to be proven."

Damn. Nicky was starting to see why Terry suspected this guy.

"Anything about Meghan Salinger in there?" Nicky asked.

"Yes, actually. Meghan tried to report him for stalking her, but it never went anywhere. He was a suspect in her disappearance but get this... the investigators on the case never even found him."

"What?" Nicky scowled. "How is that possible? Did they just give up?"

"Said he skipped town. It seems like they didn't really think he did it, because they barely looked for him."

Nicky was mad just thinking about that. She felt for Terry and Linda, and how frustrated they were with law enforcement. Nicky would do everything in her power to make sure she didn't give them the same results.

"Thanks, Grace," Nicky said. "Anything currently known about his potential location?"

"Just a sec..." More typing was heard on the other end, until Grace said, "Officially, he last worked at a garage, but we can assume he's not there anymore. Unofficially, he was seen working at a strip club, and it looks like a real skeezy place... looks like it's a couple towns over from where you're at."

Nicky looked at Ken, who nodded, clearly thinking the same thing as her.

"Send me the address, Grace."

"Will do."

Nicky hung up the phone.

She looked at Ken and said, "Looks like we're going to the strip club."

"Guess we are," Ken said.

Nicky gave a breath of relief. She knew that their work was important and that the answers they found might not turn out the way they needed them to, but she couldn't forget the emotional toll it was taking on Terry and Linda Salinger. It was a tough case, and they were going to need all the help they could get.

Seeing Linda and Terry reminded Nicky of her own parents. She and her father were long estranged, but her mother had been kind. Nicky felt a pull in her heart, a strange longing for a place that didn't exist any more.

But she snapped herself out of it. This wasn't the time for her emotions.

She needed to go up to the strip club and see what she could find out.

CHAPTER EIGHT

The drive up to the strip club was nerve-wracking for Nicky, and she didn't know what they would find when they got there. It seemed to go on forever; as she moved along the highway, the sun lowered into the horizon and painted the sky purple and orange. Ken was silent in the passenger seat.

"Should be there in ten," Nicky said.

Ken just looked outside. Nicky was finding him a bit moody, and she wondered what was on his mind. "What are you thinking about, Agent Walker?" she asked him.

He glanced at her but was quiet as he readjusted himself in the seat. "Nothing, Lyons."

"Come on," she said. "I'm not saying we need to be best friends but tell me what's on your mind. I'd like to know who my partner is."

"Fine," he said. He turned to look at her. "I'm... I'm thinking about Meghan Salinger. I feel for her parents. It's not right that they have to go through this, and I don't know how they do it. Meghan could be dead, and they have no clue. They'll never know. And the ones who were supposed to give them answers just shrugged it off and did virtually nothing. It's not justice, and that pisses me off."

Nicky nodded, listening. It seemed like that struck a personal chord for Ken.

"Is that why you became an agent?" Nicky asked. "So you could do things the right way?"

"More or less," he muttered. "What about you?"

Nicky almost laughed, shook her head. "I was trying to get to know you, Agent Walker. I'm not as much of a closed book."

He let out a bit of a laugh but said nothing else. Nicky sighed.

"It's not a secret that I was abducted when I was younger," Nicky said. "With my sister, Rosie. I got away. She didn't."

Ken was quiet. Nicky had been open about her past with her colleagues; it was all in her file anyway, and Dr. Graham had suggested that if she wasn't going to open up to friends, she should at least open up to her coworkers. It was better than keeping everything inside. And Nicky personally felt like part of being a good leader was being open and honest, rather than closed off and mysterious.

40

"That's why the senator chose me for the job," Nicky said. "I've got... personal interests in missing girls. You get that, right?"

"I do get it," Ken said. "Maybe you're not the only one with personal interests."

Nicky shot him a look, then refocused on the road. "What do you mean?"

"We're not here to investigate me," Ken said. "You want to find Meghan Salinger, don't you?"

"Of course I do. I want to see her safe."

"I feel the same way," Ken said. "So let's focus on our jobs."

Nicky nodded again. She understood that. Somebody as distant as Ken Walker wasn't going to open up so easily.

The sun had fully set now, and the blackness of the night was descending fast. The lights of the strip club were coming up, and Nicky was getting nervous. This was a dangerous man they were looking for, and when they found him, she didn't know what they'd have to face.

They pulled into the parking lot, which was half-full. Nicky parked the car and called Grace. She answered immediately. "You at the strip club?" Grace asked.

"Just got here," Nicky said. "We're outside. You sure this guy's in there?"

"Yeah, pretty sure it's him," Grace said. "I pinged the cell phone of his last known alias. He goes by Tucker here, not Darren, so keep that in mind."

"Thanks, Grace. Talk soon." Nicky hung up and stared at the strip club. It was a two-story, square-shaped building adorned with neon lights. This was definitely not the place a couple of FBI agents could just casually walk into.

Nicky glanced Ken over. He was wearing a full black casual suit, jacket and all, while she was wearing a black blouse and slacks.

"Jesus," she said, "we couldn't look more like feds. Ditch the jacket, Walker."

"What are you thinking?" He lifted an eyebrow.

"We can't go in there flashing our badges--we'll spook the guy, and he could make a run for it. We should try to blend in, at least to get past security."

Outside the door was a wide-chested bouncer with a tattoo on his bald head. Nicky had a feeling that guy wouldn't let two agents in without a fight.

Nicky flipped down the car's mirror and pulled her long, brown hair out of its ponytail, letting it fall over her shoulders. She undid a few buttons of her blouse and allowed the top of her red, lacy bra to show. Maybe it'd distract the bouncer enough for him to not notice how much of a stiff Ken was.

Ken eased his jacket off and tossed it in the back seat. "How's this?"

His hair was too perfect, too in place, so Nicky ruffled it up. Ken leaned away from her, then shot her a scowl.

"Better," she said.

With that, they got out of the car, into the warm evening. It was time to get into the club.

The bouncer eyed them as they approached the door. He was enormous and looked like he was carved out of stone. His dark eyes were focused on them, unmoving.

"ID, please," he said, his voice rough and domineering.

Nicky allowed her top to show a little more and put on a smile. "We're just trying to get in," she said.

"ID," the bouncer repeated.

Pouting, Nicky took out her wallet and slid out her ID card, then showed the bouncer.

"Wouldn't have guessed you're pushing thirty," he said, glancing at her.

Nicky gave him a pleasant smile to hide the fact that she wanted to claw his eyes out.

He checked Ken's ID too, then nodded, and allowed them to pass.

Nicky strolled into the strip club known as 'The Happy Beaver'. It was aptly named: neon, flashing lights, and scantily-clad women in animal costumes greeted her at the door. This was the type of place middle-aged men visited on their nights off to lecherously watch women dance and look at their asses. It was the type of place where the booze flowed and it was not out of the ordinary to see a fight break out.

They'd have to keep their wits about them, because one wrong move could turn this night around for the worse. Nicky didn't want herself, or Ken, to get into any fights with the crowd here. They had to find this man if they wanted to find Meghan. And they had to take him in as cleanly as possible.

Nicky spotted the bar off to the left and headed in that direction. Ken followed her, glancing around with his usual, stoic expression.

Two bartenders and a bouncer stood behind the bar, and the room was crowded. This club was packed. The music was blaring. There were two women dancing on the stage, both revealing more skin as the song went on. The first dancer wore a yellow leotard, and had a big, plastic beaver head on her head. She was writhing around the stage and giving off a sexy pout, while her partner moved erratically behind her. The second dancer wore a blue beaver head and was letting her hips grind all over the pole.

Nicky kept her head high, gaining a few looks from men by the bar. But she was only here for one reason.

Grace had forwarded Nicky a photo of Darren McMillan--or Tucker, as he was known here. She knew she was looking for a skinny, bald-headed, overly tattooed thirty-year-old. Not exactly a discreet-looking guy, and Nicky couldn't help but wonder why the hell the previous investigators had given up on him so quickly. Nicky had never seen a father more certain than Terry had been that Darren was responsible for Meghan's disappearance.

As Nicky scanned the sea of faces, she spotted a woman by the bar--and a guy who looked just like Darren was leaning over her. The woman had long, flowing red hair, just like Meghan's. In fact, she looked so much like her that Nicky nearly had a heart attack.

The entire case almost fell on top of her head. For a moment, she thought maybe, Meghan was right here, alive, and she'd run off with Darren...

But then the girl turned her head to the side. She had a much longer nose.

Damn. This wasn't Meghan Salinger. But that guy was definitely Darren McMillan.

"There he is," Nicky said to Ken.

"Oh, I see him," Ken said. "How do you wanna do this?"

"We don't want to let him know we're FBI, not yet."

Ken nodded. "Agreed."

"You stay here," Nicky said. "I'll go to the bar and get a drink, then say hello and see what happens. If I can get him to come with me, I'll bring him outside somewhere quiet."

"What if he's not willing?" Ken asked.

Nicky paused, her eyes skating over Darren. He wasn't a small guy, but she'd been trained for this. "Then I'll take him down."

"Let's hope it doesn't come to that," Ken said.

"Just back me up," Nicky said. "If you see me corner him, that's your cue. We need to back him into a wall so he can't run."

With that, Nicky made her way to the bar. Her heart was beating fast. She didn't know why exactly. There was something about this guy that was just... off. It was something else, something she couldn't place. All she knew was that something about him just wasn't right, and Nicky had a feeling he could turn out to be a genuinely dangerous man.

The woman next to him was laughing. Nicky opened her mouth to ask for a drink, but before she could, she heard Darren say, "Damn, baby, let's get out of here."

The girl with Darren giggled. "You're bad, Tucker. I don't know..."

"Come on, let's do this."

"Well... okay."

Nicky had to act fast. She stumbled over to the bar and pretended to be drunk, bumping right into the girl Darren was with. Nicky squealed and spilled a drink all over Darren, who let out a guttural sound.

"What the hell!" Darren yelled. He looked like he was about to eat Nicky's face off--until he took in her appearance. Blatantly, in front of his date, he scanned Nicky up and down. "Damn, you're new here," he said.

Nicky got close to him. "Hey," she said alluringly. She glanced over her shoulder. Ken was closing in.

"We're a little busy here," Darren's date said to Nicky. "Do you mind?"

Nicky felt bad for the girl, who was probably just a normal person in this situation--but at the same time, Nicky knew Darren had been linked to human trafficking before. She wasn't about to let this girl's life get taken away, not on her watch.

Nicky needed to get Darren's attention away from this girl, and she needed to do it fast.

She hated doing this, but she turned to the date and gave her a sour look. "Sorry, sweetheart, but I think you're in over your head. Why don't you go find another date? This one's mine."

The girl's jaw dropped while Darren looked at Nicky with a sickening smile. The girl looked at Nicky, then back at Darren, a scowl on her face. Darren just shrugged and said, "You heard the lady. Beat it."

The girl stormed off in the opposite direction, pissed and hurt. But she had no idea that her life had probably just been saved.

Nicky looked at Darren with her best flirty expression, and he scanned her up and down in a sickening way. She was backing him into the bar, and they were near a corner--which meant it wouldn't be too easy for Darren to get away. She could feel Ken looming near her.

"You're feisty," Darren said. He flashed her his teeth, which had gold grills on them. A giant tattoo of a rose with thorns covered his pale-skinned neck. "I like that."

Nicky wanted to hurl. "Gee, thanks, baby," she said.

She couldn't play this up for long. She went in to grab Darren's arm. At first, he thought she was flirting. He wore a big, gross smile.

But then Nicky yanked him in close. She stole a glance in her periphery to see Ken was there and ready.

She looked Darren dead in the eye and said: "FBI, dirtbag. You're coming with us."

Then it all happened at once. Darren started to move--but then Ken grabbed him from behind and held him tight. It was too late for Darren to make a run for it.

People at the bar were starting to look at them. Nicky feared for a second that Darren was going to produce a gun--but then the other patrons turned back to their drinks, not wanting to get involved.

"Let's go," Nicky said. "Walk."

Darren twisted his arm until he broke free from Ken's grip. He went to run off, but Ken grabbed him by the arm again—only for Darren to elbow him in the face.

"Hey!" Nicky yelled.

But Darren had escaped. He dove through the strip club, dodging past people.

Game on.

Nicky dove after him. He was a lot faster than she had anticipated. She was just about to grab him by the collar when Darren turned around and kicked her right in the face.

Nicky stumbled backwards. She got her balance back and started to run. Darren was darting through the crowd. His head was literally bobbing up and down. He bumped into three people, who yelped and spilled their drinks.

But Darren didn't seem to care. He continued his mad dash across the club, darting for the staircase that led up to the second floor.

Ken was right behind him. He was yelling, "Federal agent! Stop, McMillan!"

Darren darted up the stairs. Nicky and Ken chased after, weaving between people the best they could. The music kept pounding Nicky's ears.

On the upper level, Nicky saw Darren run into a room. "There!" she shouted to Ken.

Both of them ran right in after him. But Darren was pulling open a window. He looked over his shoulder at them. There was no way he was going to jump, Nicky reasoned—but on his face was the look of a man who would do anything to escape.

"Don't even think about it," Nicky warned.

45

"No," Darren said. "No way. I'm not going to jail."

"Darren—"

He jumped out of the window.

For a second, Nicky was worried he'd killed himself just to escape. But she and Ken rushed over and looked down. Darren was inside of a dumpster, and hauling himself out of it, and Nicky's resolve burned back to life.

"He's gonna get away!" Nicky shouted.

She couldn't let that happen. And Ken must have sensed her plan, because he said, "Lyons, don't you--"

Too late.

Nicky jumped out of the window. A rush of adrenaline surged through her chest, and she landed with a hard thud in the dumpster, surrounded by stinking filth. It hurt a bit, but she was fine.

She tore out of the dumpster and got herself back on the ground. Ken wasn't behind her, but she didn't care.

She darted after Darren.

He was sprinting along the alleyway, looking over his shoulder every so often to see if Nicky was following. She wouldn't let him go, her feet pounding the pavement below.

"Stop and put your hands up!" Nicky shouted.

Darren was at the end of the alley. There was a street up ahead. He wasn't getting away, and Nicky was closing in fast.

But then a car screeched down the street. Nicky reached out to grab Darren, but the car honked and blocked her way. The driver was a well-dressed asshole in a suit. He flipped her off.

"Damn it," Nicky said. She looked over at Darren, who was running down the street as fast as he could. She chased after him.

Darren made it onto the sidewalk, but his foot caught on something and he tripped, falling to the ground. Nicky stormed up to him, shouting, "Darren McMillan, stop! You're under arrest!"

Fumbling to his feet, he reached into his pants--and pulled out a knife. "Oh, hell no! I'll kill you, bitch!"

Nicky stopped where she was. On instinct, her hand went for her gun—but something stopped her. Flashbacks from Frank, the man who'd took Masie, flashed through her mind. Nicky didn't want another repeat, but Darren was facing off against her, knife gleaming in the street lights.

"Stay back!" he yelled, his arm shaking. "Come any closer and I'll—"

Suddenly, Darren froze.

There were footsteps behind them. Startled, Nicky looked over her shoulder to see Ken hurrying over with his gun out, pointed right at Darren. Darren's hands flew up, and he dropped the knife.

Relief flowed through her. They could apprehend him without gunshots being involved—thank God for that. Nicky pulled her cuffs out and walked over to a now trembling Darren. As Ken kept the gun on him, Nicky grabbed Darren's wrists and slapped cuffs on him.

He was caught, and no one had to die for it.

CHAPTER NINE

Nicky stared Darren McMillan dead in the eyes in the interrogation room at the local police station. It was a cramped, windowless purgatory with a metal table and a dirty mirror on the wall, and it was cold and dingier than what Nicky was used to, but it would have to do.

Across from her and Ken, Darren McMillan was cuffed and sitting on a chair, but he looked like a rabid dog.

He wanted out. He wanted revenge against Nicky. He was going to kill her.

"I want a law—"

He was definitely about to say "lawyer," but Nicky cut him off before he could finish. "I want to know about Meghan Salinger," Nicky said. Ken shot Nicky a look.

"Who do you think you are, huh?" Darren rambled. "You're nothing! You can't keep me here; you've got nothing on me."

Ken rested his hands on the table. "McMillan, you need to calm down and answer our questions. You drew a knife on a federal agent. That itself is a serious offense."

Darren was seething. He wanted to rip their heads off, Nicky could tell.

"Fuck that bitch Meghan," he said. "I'm over her."

"Is that what you said when you kidnapped her?" Nicky quipped.

Darren scowled. "I had nothin' to do with that!"

Nicky scoffed. "You expect us to believe that?" She slammed her fist on the table. "You were stalking her, Darren. And then you ran away from the cops."

"I didn't run away!" he shouted. "I already talked to the cops, damn it. Don't you people have access to all that stuff?"

Nicky and Ken exchanged an uneasy look. Nowhere in Darren's file had it said that the cops had found him, at all. If he was telling the truth--that meant the FBI somehow did not receive the report from the police.

Or the police never filed it.

"Look, I told that other cop," Darren rambled, "I had nothing to do with Meghan disappearing. She probably took off on her own, okay?

Besides, it's like I told him--I have an alibi for the other chick, so I'm innocent."

Nicky paused. "What 'other chick?'" This case was getting more confusing by the second.

"The other chick who went missing! That cop I talked to--I forget his name. Rawlings? Rawley? Ryley? I dunno, but there was another chick he said went missing under the exact same situation as Meghan and I could prove I didn't do that one, so I was cleared, okay?"

Nicky's head reeled. There was a chance Darren was making all of this up.

"Did that cop give you a name on that other victim?" Nicky pressed.

"I don't remember," Darren spat.

"Think harder," Ken demanded.

"No, I'm not going to think any harder," he snapped. "I already told you what I know--"

"And we already know you lied." Ken pulled out a file and slapped it on the table. "You were stalking Meghan. You were obsessed with her."

"Oh, I was obsessed, was I?" Darren laughed. "Meghan was an emotional basket case. She was crazy. She was trying to leave me and I wouldn't let her, big fuckin' deal."

"You mean when she tried to leave you and break up with you," Nicky said, "you got violent."

"I'm violent to everybody," Darren said. "Get away from me. I don't want to be near you."

"Tell me the name of the other victim," Nicky said.

"I don't remember."

"Bullshit."

Ken swiped his hand through the air. "Look, Darren, let's just cut to the chase. We know you've been linked to human trafficking before, and you managed to sneak your way out of charges. But you're not going to get away with it this time."

"I already told you this, you piece of shit," Darren snapped. "I didn't remember the name of that other chick, okay? Maybe it was Stacey or Sarah or something. Doesn't matter. I didn't do anything to her, and I didn't do anything to Meghan."

Nicky leaned in. Her eyes darted back and forth, taking in Darren's face. As dirty as this guy seemed, he did appear to be telling the truth. But if that were the case, then that would make this all even more confusing. If Darren talked to the police and was cleared of any wrongdoing, then why was it never filed?

"Where did this Rawlings or whoever cop work?" Nicky asked. "Do you know?"

"It was back in Frankstown. I'm tellin' you, talk to them and this'll all get sorted out."

"We don't have any record of the police talking to you," Nicky said.

"So maybe the cops back there don't file a report if I didn't actually do anything," Darren said.

Nicky frowned. It was possible that was true, but then that would mean these cops were dirty.

"Are you sure about that, Darren?" Nicky asked. "Are you really sure you didn't do anything to Meghan or this other girl? If you just hurt one woman, that means you got away with it once, which means you would probably do it again."

Darren was seething, shaking in his chair. "How many times do I gotta repeat myself?" he said. His tone was no longer jocular and borderline maniacal. It was quiet, reserved, and angry. "Let me out of here. You've got nothing on me."

"You're not going anywhere, Darren," Nicky said.

"I'm not talking to you anymore," Darren said. "You people don't have shit on me; you can't keep me here."

"For pulling a knife on a federal agent, we can," Ken said.

Nicky stood, skidding her chair against the floor. "Stay here and think about what you've done, Darren."

With that, she breezed to the door, Ken behind her. They left Darren thrashing like a wild animal in the interrogation room and reconvened outside. They were in a small, cramped police station not far from the strip club, but if what Darren said was true, then they needed to get back to Frankstown and hunt down this Rawling or Ryley character. But first: Nicky needed to confirm whether any of it was true.

They went into the lobby of the police station, where an older secretary sat behind the desk. She looked up at Nicky and Ken through her glasses. "You two find what you're lookin' for with that guy?"

"Actually," Nicky said, "we were wondering if you could give us any information on a cop over in Frankstown. Should be in your database, right?"

The secretary nodded, going on her computer. "Yeah, should have it. What's the name?"

"Should be something like Ryley or Rawling, something with an R."

The secretary typed in the name and waited. "Nothing's coming up," she said.

Ken ran his hand across his hair. "Are you sure?"

"Certain," the secretary said. "I . . . oh," she said, looking at the computer screen.

"What is it?" Nicky said.

The secretary swallowed and looked up. "I'm getting a picture of a police officer named Rawley in Frankstown--"

"That's the one," Ken said.

"--but it looks like he was let go from his position three months ago."

"What for?" Nicky asked. This case was seriously starting to stink.

"Soliciting prostitution," the secretary said. "Seems like he was a dirty cop."

Nicky looked at Ken. He gave her a steely gaze that said he was thinking the same thing: this had corruption written all over it.

"Anything else you can tell me about him?" Nicky asked. "Did he ever have anything to do with any missing persons reports?"

The secretary scrolled down her screen, which was reflected in her glasses. "There's not much on him or his history here. You'd have to go down to Frankstown if you want to know more."

Nicky looked at Ken and nodded. "I guess we should pay them a visit."

***

The moment Nicky walked into the Frankstown police station, she could smell the corruption. It was a dirty little police station, with its cracked paint and stains all over the floor, the walls decorated with an incoherent collection of posters and some of the worst paintings she had ever seen. Nicky could see the smug look of superiority among the police officers. At one desk was a large man with a belly the size of a house. He was laughing with another officer, but even from here, Nicky could see the disdain in his eyes.

They all went quiet as Nicky and Ken made their way in. They'd fixed their disguises from earlier so they were looking like normal agents again, and surely, these cops could smell that from a mile away.

The oversized police officer got up, looking down at them and sneering. "Yeah?"

"Hello, I'm Agent Nicky Lyons," Nicky said, showing her badge as she walked up to his desk. "This is my partner, Agent Ken Walker."

"I'm Sheriff Corbin. Feds, huh?" he said, his voice hostile. "What brings you here?"

"We're here to talk to you about a man named Rawley," Ken said.

"I'm not sure what you're referring to." Corbin sat on his desk, crossing his arms over his barrel chest.

"We need to talk about a certain missing person's case. A woman named Sarah Mills," Nicky said. On the way over here, Nicky had asked Ken to dig into the alleged missing woman Darren was talking about, and he had come up with Sarah Mills. However, there wasn't much information on the case in the database, according to Ken.

"What about it?"

"We would like to know the details of the case. Based on our intel, it was in your jurisdiction. An officer named Rawley was on the case before he was discharged."

"I'm not sure what you're talking about," Corbin said.

Nicky's jaw clenched. Why was he being so stubborn? "We know your precinct was working on a case involving Sarah Mills. Why did it go nowhere?"

The sheriff leaned back and laughed, his belly jiggling. "Now, why would I do that, darlin'? The Feds are just a bunch of pencil pushers anyway."

Nicky's blood boiled. She and Ken knew this was the kind of cop that never would have passed the FBI training. The kind of cop that would have been thrown out the first day. She took a deep breath.

"Sheriff Corbin, I don't appreciate your attitude," she said.

"You need to watch yourself, little girl," Corbin said. "I don't take to smart talkin' from women and I sure as hell don't take to Feds messin' around in my police station."

Nicky's blood was burning. She was about to bite back when Ken stepped in.

"If you aren't willing to cooperate with the FBI, we can bring the man upstairs down here to deal with you," Ken said, "and expose this station of yours for its corruption."

The sheriff didn't even blink. "I don't see any cameras in here."

Nicky glanced around. He was right. There were no cameras in sight.

But then the sheriff let out a belly laugh. "Relax. You stiffs always take everything so seriously. I'm messing with ya."

Nicky wasn't laughing, and neither was Ken.

"Sheriff Corbin," Nicky said, "why don't we go down to the station's archives and look at Sarah Mills's case file."

Corbin didn't move. "I don't think so."

Nicky's fists clenched. "Why not?"

"It's not in there," Corbin said. "You're barking up the wrong tree."

"If you don't show us that case file," Ken said, "we'll go upstairs and your superiors will hear about all the corrupt things that go on in this station."

Corbin laughed. "My superiors?" he said, his voice jovial yet mocking. "I don't think you know who you're dealing with, son. I'm the one who runs this station."

Nicky's nails dug into her palms. This guy was getting under her skin, and she was losing patience trying to be professional. "Just hand over the case file," Nicky said.

Corbin glared at her for a long moment before he sighed and stood up. "All right, girly, calm yourself. Let's go to the filing room."

He led them down a long hallway to a room lined with file cabinets on either side. There wasn't a single camera in sight, but Corbin was right: they were definitely in the right place.

Corbin walked over to the filing cabinet, pulling it open and taking out a folder. "Sarah Mills's case file," he said, dropping it on the table in front of them.

Nicky opened it up.

And in it was a photo of a red-headed woman who looked strikingly similar to Meghan Salinger. Ken looked over Nicky's shoulder at the file but said nothing. He didn't need to.

Nicky leafed through the papers. Sarah Mills was a twenty-two-year-old girl who married young, who wanted to grow up and become an actress. Her story somewhat mirrored Meghan's, although Meghan was older, twenty-four, and was an aspiring singer who had already found a bit of fame.

"Got what you need?" the sheriff grunted.

"Yeah. We'll be taking this," Nicky said. She straightened up and looked the sheriff dead in his eyes to intimidate him, show him that the FBI was not to be messed with. "And Sheriff, I suggest you make sure these reports get sent in next time. I'd hate to see you lose your job over negligence."

"You have a nice day now," Corbin said, but his voice was apathetic.

With that, Nicky and Ken left the Frankstown police station. It was warm outside, but late, with the stars now shining down on them. Nicky and Ken stood under a streetlamp.

"Damn, it's late," Ken said. "Any idea where we're staying?"

Nicky gripped the file in her hand, her head still back in that police station. "Guess we need to find a motel."

Nicky sighed, stared up at the night sky for a moment. She hated sleeping anywhere but her own bed, but she had a feeling she wouldn't be doing much sleeping anyway--not with this case on her mind.

CHAPTER TEN

Nicky couldn't believe what she was hearing.

"We've only got one room." The curmudgeonly old lady behind the counter at the motel reeked of perfume and cigarettes. Not to mention the motel lobby itself was beyond shabby. The motel was a skip and a jump from being condemned. Dusty, peeling wallpaper, mold in the corners, a chipped linoleum floor. The old lady behind the counter had a smile that showed only one row of yellow teeth. She sat at her post with a cigarette hanging out of her mouth, strands of hair coming out of her gray bun, her makeup slathered on to hide the wrinkles.

"Well, we need two," Ken told her firmly.

Clearly, he didn't want to share a room with Nicky either. Nicky was in agreement with him there. They'd been coworkers for a short period of time, but they'd never gotten along or worked one-on-one. Sharing a room sounded beyond awkward.

"Well, too bad," the lady said. "That's all we've got."

Ken's brow arched. "And what if we refuse to pay for one room and decide to find a different motel?"

The lady laughed. "You can stay out there all night for all I care." She pulled out the pack of cigarettes from her breast pocket and lit another one, sucking in a deep breath.

Nicky glanced over at Ken and sighed. She didn't want to share a room either, but this was her job and she needed to be professional. It wasn't like they'd have to sleep in the same bed—Nicky could crash on the floor if she had to.

"We'll take it," Nicky said. "We'll just share."

Ken's brow arched. "Really?"

"We'll just be sleeping," Nicky said, "I promise I won't kill you in your sleep. There has to be a couch or something."

"I think it's got a futon," the lady grumbled.

Nicky and Ken exchanged a look, then they stepped aside and waited for the lady to pull out their room key.

"Room 214," she said, sliding the key across the counter. "I hope you two enjoy yourselves." She winked. "And don't forget to bring me back a souvenir."

The key was just a plain old piece of plastic with a number on it. Nicky and Ken then grabbed their bags and headed for the stairs, which led to the second floor. Nicky felt a chill as she walked up the stairs, staring at the threadbare carpeting that stuck to her feet.

"A futon?" Ken asked as they walked into the room. It was just as shabby as the lobby, if not worse, with lace curtains that hung from the window, a chipping laminate countertop, and a stained carpet.

"Well," Nicky said, "it'll save us a bit of money."

Ken placed his bag on the bed, which was just a mattress laid on the floor, and leaned against the wall. "It's safer this way," he said. "If anything happens, we'll know. You take the bed."

Nicky looked at Ken slyly. "You're a gentleman, Agent Walker, but really, I can take the couch. You're an old man, after all."

He grunted. "I'm thirty-five. And my mother would kill me if she found out I let a woman sleep on the couch."

Nicky smiled. "Who knew you had a gentlemanly side, Agent Walker?"

He just grunted again, saying nothing. Nicky laughed, then began unpacking her belongings in the bathroom. It was a moment of levity that she needed.

This case was too much for her. She knew that even considering it would be a bad idea. And yet she'd gone ahead and gotten pulled into it anyway. This was her chance to redeem herself and show her colleagues that she was still a strong FBI agent and that she wasn't just washed-up and incapable of saving anyone.

She was desperate. She wanted to save those girls. But she was also uneasy. She couldn't deny that she was afraid--afraid that this case would be unlike anything she'd ever experienced before. Afraid that she'd fail, like she'd failed Masie.

Like she'd failed Rosie.

Nicky brushed that thought away. She didn't want to get emotional, not in front of Ken. She didn't want to be perceived as weak.

She changed into pajamas and went back into the main room. Ken was already on the futon, his back facing her. Saying nothing, Nicky crawled into the bed. It was stiff and smelled moldy. Nasty. But it would have to do.

Accepting her fate, she lay on the pillow, shut her eyes, and let herself drift away.

***

When Nicky awoke, she was sixteen again.

The van grumbled beneath her. She looked around, startled, before her surroundings set in. The smell of mildew. The coffee stain on the seat beside her. The hula girl on the dashboard...

And Rosie beside her in the back.

The man, driving in the front, the sunset filtering through the windshield.

Nicky didn't know it then. But she knew it now, as an outsider looking back in.

He was taking them to the lake house.

He drove them deep into the woods, through a narrow trail. The stones popped and tinged beneath the wheels of the car. Fear pounded in Nicky's chest. She wanted to open the door, to jump out with Rosie, but the man still held that gun as he drove. If they made any sudden moves, he could end their lives in an instant.

Nicky looked at Rosie. She would never forget the fear in her sister's brown eyes. Rosie was a year younger than Nicky, and she had always been more naive. While Nicky liked to date boys in town, drink alcohol sometimes and party, Rosie was bookish and smart. But they were best friends. Nicky would have died for her.

The man stopped the car outside of a lake. It was dark now, navy blue taking over the world. When he shut off the headlights, the only light that shone down was from the full moon above.

As Nicky's eyes adjusted, she saw that they were also parked beside an old, derelict cabin, right in front of the lake.

Nicky and Rosie were both shaking, terrified. Nicky remembered feeling like it was all a sick, twisted dream. A nightmare. This summer was supposed to be about having fun with her friends and her sister. Just last night, Nicky and Rosie had been out at the old playground with a group of people; Nicky got a little tipsy off the alcohol some of the older boys had brought, while Rosie had obviously stayed sober. Rosie was the younger one, but she was also the responsible one, and she'd always keep an eye on Nicky if she ever got too drunk.

But it was all going to end. They were both going to die.

The man kept the gun on them and directed them to the edge of the lake. He watched them, smiling, before he tied their hands with rope. Nicky didn't struggle against the restraints. She was too petrified.

"Do you know what I'm going to do?" he asked.

Nicky felt her chest tightening. She didn't want to look. She didn't want to see.

"I'm going to throw you in the water," he said.

And he did.

Nicky plunged into dark, cold water. Bubbles fizzled up toward the surface, where she could see the moonlight filtering in. She kicked and struggled, but without her hands, she just couldn't swim.

She was going to die here.

She was sure, in that moment, that it was all over.

***

Nicky awoke with a gasp, drenched in sweat. It took her mind a moment to realize she wasn't back at the lake. She was in a motel room.

There was a voice: "Lyons, are you okay?"

Nicky jolted out of her trance and looked over. Ken was sitting on the edge of her bed, his thick, dark eyebrows furrowed. His hands were hovering over her. Then it hit her--she must have been vocal in her sleep. Vocal about the nightmare--no, the memory--that still hung so heavy on her mind.

The lake.

Rosie...

It was all too real.

"Lyons," Ken said. He placed a gentle hand on her arm.

In her right mind, Nicky would be horrified to be so close to Ken Walker, of all people, but not only that--her colleague was seeing her in a truly vulnerable moment. She would be mortified by it later. But right now, the panic was too strong. Her heart pounded in her ears. She couldn't escape the images. She felt like she was still at the bottom of that lake. Like she'd never really left.

Nicky hugged herself and pinched her eyes shut, trying desperately to hold back her sobs.

Her psychiatrist had been over this with her a million times. Her PTSD from the incident sometimes sent her right back in time, to the point where she had no control over how she might act or feel in the present moment.

After a moment, she felt Ken's hand on her shoulder squeeze. She hated herself for being comforted by it. Hated herself because she needed this. To feel close to another person. She couldn't help it. She let herself lean onto him, feel the warmth of him, even if this was Ken, of all people. Nicky didn't care. At least she was able to keep it together long enough to not cry.

"I'm sorry," she said, pulling away, but she couldn't stop the trembling.

58

"No," Ken said softly. "Don't apologize. It's okay. Where were you?"

After this embarrassing display, the least she could do was be honest. "It's... about what happened with my sister. I relive it sometimes. That's all."

Ken nodded. "I've read your file, Lyons. I know what happened. I'm sorry."

"It's okay," Nicky said. "I'm sorry I woke you up."

"No. It's fine. I'm glad you did. I'm glad I was there."

Nicky's brow furrowed, but she didn't want to ask. Once she did, she'd have to remember she was talking to Ken Walker. She wasn't sure if she could handle that.

"Can I ask you something?" she said instead.

"Sure."

"What are you doing here? I mean, why'd you become a profiler? Why'd you join the FBI?" It was an excuse to know him more, but also to veer the conversation away from herself.

Her question must have caught him off-guard. He took a moment to choose his answer. Nicky felt a twinge of guilt for prying, but she had to know.

"I joined the FBI because I want to catch the monsters of the world," he said. "I want to stop them before they kill more people."

"A noble cause," Nicky said.

"It isn't just that, though. I think... I think I want people to remember the victims of these cases," Ken explained. "I think I want to honor them for who they were, and who they became. I want them to matter. I want people to know that they were real, legitimate people with stories and backgrounds..."

"But why? What motivates you, personally?"

Ken hesitated a moment, but then nodded. "I told you before, you're not the only one with personal interests in cases like this. When I was a teenager, there was this... girl. I'm gonna have to get sappy on you for a moment, but she was the first 'crush' I ever had. Yeah, I know it sounds kiddish now, but back then it was everything."

Nicky nodded. "I get it. When you're a teenager, you feel everything. I remember those days." Her heart sank as she thought about that last night she'd spent with Rosie and all their friends, the night before Rosie went missing.

"Yeah, well. I ended up convincing this girl to give me a shot, and we started dating. Long story short, it worked out, and we were together until senior year."

A lump grew in Nicky's throat. She had a bad feeling that she knew where this was going.

"Then prom night happened," Ken said, "and Tiana—that was her name—was supposed to meet me there. She was running late and didn't want me to miss out on the limo with our friends."

It was hard to picture Ken Walker being a normal teenager once, but Nicky could see it all. It brought her back to her own days in high school, when she'd left everyone she ever knew behind. There were a lot of conflicting emotions. The message from Matt slipped back into her mind, but she swiped it away, listening to Ken's story.

"Anyway, hours passed at prom," Ken said, "and Tiana—she never showed up. I'll skip all the in-between details and just tell you that no one ever saw her alive again. The police said it seemed likely she was abducted on her way over to prom, as she was walking there." His face grew serious, and he couldn't meet Nicky's eyes. "They found her body two weeks later. The guy who did it was caught within a couple of months. He was just some drifter, saw Tiana in her prom dress and thought she'd be an easy target because she was alone." He laughed sullenly. "Guess he was right."

Nicky's mind was a jumble of thoughts and emotions. "I'm so sorry," she said. "That's horrible." But now she understood. She understood why this case had such a hold on Ken.

Their stories were different, but in the end, their motivations were the same.

They wanted to save the girls who needed to be saved.

He was quiet for a long time. "Nothing I can ever do will bring her back. So I just try to save as many people as I can while I'm still here."

Nicky understood that. At the same time, in her case, Rosie's body had never been found. And so Nicky still held onto that hope that someday, she'd find her.

Still, Nicky couldn't believe Ken had opened up. She could hardly believe that this was the same cold, distant Agent Walker she'd known at the office. He had a compassionate side.

She also knew the way things could get intense during the night. Emotions were high. Maybe it was biological. She remembered her fling with Fernando--it had started off as lust. Nicky had needs, and hookup apps always felt too risky for her--too high of a risk of predators. She and Fernando had worked too closely together on a case. Then Fernando caught feelings for Nicky and she couldn't give him what he wanted. In fact, he became more annoying to her than anything else.

She looked up at Ken to see him still staring at her. She shuffled back, as if to remind him of their position. Ken must have taken the hint, because he awkwardly backed off.

They were both reminded that they barely knew each other.

They had each opened up a window to each other, and Nicky knew they'd regret it in the morning.

"Well... goodnight," Nicky said.

Ken stood up, wiped his palms on his pants. "Get some sleep, Lyons. You need it."

Nicky rested her head against the pillow.

He was right. She did need sleep.

She needed to be in her right mind to catch the kidnapper. And tomorrow, Nicky wouldn't waste any time.

Whoever is doing this should be scared, Nicky thought.

Because she was coming for him. And she would take him down.

CHAPTER ELEVEN

He had given her a bed. A dresser. A vanity with a mirror and a brush so she could do her hair and look pretty for him. He had given her everything a woman could ever ask for.

The screen illuminated the dark room, giving him a full view of his bride on the other side. She was sitting at the edge of the bed, her hands clenched into fists and her eyes tightly closed. She was crying bitterly, her tears flowing like a waterfall down her face. She was crying for a freedom that he'd taken from her. It was as if he had ripped her heart out and stomped on it, crushing it beneath his feet.

He hoped once they wed, she would be more grateful for all he'd given her. She could not leave the bedroom--of course not, he knew she would run. He smiled at the screen and leaned closer. He didn't interact with her much when she was awake; their beautiful conversations would be saved for when they were officially married.

Soon, she would give up on her pacing and crying and go to bed. Then, he would get to smell her, touch her, feel her...

He watched the screen as she got under the covers and turned off the lamp. He rose from his chair and left his room, making his way down the hallway to hers. In the darkness of the hallway, he could barely make out the line where the carpet ended, and the hardwood floor began. The floor was cool underneath his bare feet. He could hear the sound of her breathing in his mind, slow and steady and deep. It was like a lullaby. He wanted to hear her breaths for real.

He reached her door. Several locks kept her in, and he unlatched them, one by one.

Inside, the room was dark. The only window was at the top of the room, and it allowed a silvery beam of moonlight to sneak in and illuminate her sleeping form. She was so beautiful.

He could see her chest rising and falling. The thin blanket bunched around her waist, exposing the rest of her body.

His palms began to sweat, and he stepped into the room.

She exhaled, and he froze in place, watching to see if she would wake up. She didn't. He sat at the edge of her bed. Her long hair tickled his arm as he did so. If she was awake, she was not responding to him. But that was okay.

"Shh," he whispered, stroking her hair. He felt her stiffen beneath him.

He smiled and continued to pet her hair. He ran his fingers through it, relishing the softness. He ran his hands over her arms and down them, feeling the thin layer of her nightgown.

She was so warm.

His hand moved to her shoulder, and, then, to her chest.

She continued to breathe, pretending to be unaware of his touch. But he knew she was awake. He knew she could feel him.

He ran his hands over her flat stomach, then her hip, then her thigh.

She didn't move.

He brought his face closer to hers, and he could smell her. It was the most beautiful odor he had ever encountered. Rich and sweet, it made his nose curl up.

He buried his face in her hair and inhaled more of her essence.

It only made her smell sweeter, and she smelled incredible. He breathed her in, as he slipped his hand inside the thin fabric of her nightgown.

She gasped and stiffened, but she stayed put.

The feel of her skin sent him into a frenzy. His fingers moved over her stomach, down her hip, and under her leg. Her thigh was soft and smooth. His fingers brushed against her hipbone, over her ribs, and up to the part of her where the fabric dipped.

She whimpered again. This time, he was sure she was awake.

His hand moved to her neck, and he pushed the blanket away from her shoulders. He moved his hands over her chest, feeling the skin against his fingertips, and he could feel her heart beating against his palm.

The room was silent, but he felt he could hear her heartbeat. It was so strong, so intoxicating.

But he stopped himself there. He had to. He couldn't give into temptation, not yet. It was too soon. He had to earn her first. And she had to earn him.

"Don't worry, my love," he said, letting her go. "Our time will come soon. Just you wait..."

With that, he got up and left the room, making sure each lock was secured shut on his way out.

He returned to his own room and sighed, pressing his back to the door.

He was proud of himself for being so strong. He smiled and continued to watch the screen, a smile on his face as he watched her sleep.

"I'm so proud of you," he said softly. "So proud."

He picked up the large red marker off his desk and went to the calendar, marking off another day done, another day closer to their big day. He grinned, feeling warm.

Only a few more days, and she would be his forever.

CHAPTER TWELVE

Nicky pressed her foot on the gas pedal, the engine roaring as the car rapidly gained speed. The road was straight and the pavement was smooth, the tires gripping the asphalt. Beside her in the passenger seat, Ken was silently reviewing Sarah Mills's file.

They hadn't talked about last night, and Nicky had no intentions of bringing it up. It was awkward as hell. The whole morning, they'd been quietly tiptoeing around each other, but the weight of it all hung in the air. Nicky just wanted to focus on her job, and not think about how she'd lost herself in her panic. She didn't want to think about how Ken's hand on her shoulder had made her feel safe, or how in the dead of night, they'd opened their hearts to each other, just a little.

They were on their way to Sarah Mills's husband's house. Well, according to the file, it was more like a trailer. But it was a bit of a drive out.

"I still can't believe those idiots," Nicky said to fill the silence. Ken glanced over at her, so she continued. "The negligence of it all. Not properly reporting this case. If it is related to Meghan, it could change everything."

"I don't expect much more from cops like that," Ken said. "They probably just wanted to close the case and move on."

"But Sarah Mills was never found," Nicky said. "Why even become a cop if you don't want to save lives?"

"Maybe they're just in it for the paycheck."

"And the pension?"

Ken shrugged.

"It's a good thing we're here to fix that," Nicky said. "Let's hope she's still alive."

Ken sighed. "You really think she is?"

"We'll find out soon enough."

The car lurched and bounced over the terrain as Nicky drove, following the GPS's directions. The dirt road was rough, poorly maintained. The car's tires crunched over the gravel as it made its way through the forest. The trees were tall and green, and the sunlight filtered through the leaves and dappled the road with a warm glow.

65

When it said to turn left, Nicky slowed the car down and looked both ways. The road was bumpy and narrow, and she could see the trees on both sides of it. A canopy of branches blocked out the sun, turning the air gray and cold.

"This is the address?" Ken asked skeptically.

"That's what it says..."

Beneath the wheels of the car, Nicky could feel the ground getting mushier and wetter. It was like they were driving right into a swamp.

"You sure we're on the right road, Lyons?" Ken asked.

Nicky was focused on trying to keep the steering wheel straight, but she felt herself losing control. "Yes, Walker, this is the right road," she said, irritated.

The trees crowded closer, their branches snaking across the road until Nicky couldn't see anything but leaves on either side.

Okay, maybe they were a bit off track. The GPS on the car's screen said they were on the right road, but Nicky was beginning to feel more nervous by the moment. She didn't like the idea of admitting Ken's hesitance had been right. But at the same time, she didn't want to get stuck in the swamplands.

"I think we should turn around," Nicky said, although she was still driving forward.

But it was too late--the car was already slowing down.

"What's going on, Lyons?" Ken asked.

A surge of panic hit Nicky's chest. She couldn't control the car. "I don't know!"

The car stopped with a jolt, and Nicky slammed her foot on the gas, but it was useless. The tires just spun in the mud.

"Shit," Ken said. Sweat creased his brow. "Okay. You keep trying to go forward. I'll go push and see if I can get us out."

The window looked out on a murky swamp below. The water was dark, and the trees were so close that their branches brushed against the glass. All around them, the swamp was filled with tall reeds and murky water. Nicky could see the mud and the muck on the bottom of the swamp. So much for the "road."

"Walker, you're going to get dirty as hell."

"What other choice do I have?" Ken said.

He got out of the car and went to the back of it. Nicky kept spinning the wheels. Through the rear-view mirror, Nicky saw Ken try to push the car, but the tires just kept spinning in place, sending mud flinging in all directions.

Nicky sighed, pressed her forehead to the steering wheel. This was just her luck.

But Ken wasn't giving up. She felt the car jolt. Ken shoved harder. And all at once, the car lurched forward.

Nicky's head snapped up so fast she nearly gave herself whiplash.

Ken had stopped pushing and was now leaning back against the car's trunk. He was hunched over, his arms resting on his knees, his breathing ragged. His shirt was already covered in mud. He was so close. She could see the sweat on his forehead, the lines of strain around his eyes, and the way his chest heaved with each breath.

"What happened?" Nicky asked.

Ken shook his head. "I dunno, I pushed and the car just started moving forward." He wiped his brow. "You should be able to drive us out of here now."

"Just as long as we're not going backwards," Nicky said. "Guess we've gotta find another way out."

She put her foot on the gas and let the car roll forward. Through the rear-view mirror, she watched as the trees pressed against her car, the branches scraping at her windows.

As far as nightmares went, this was up there for Nicky. The deeper they got into the brush, the more trapped she felt.

It reminded her too much of that night, all those years ago, with Rosie, as the man had driven them to the lake house. Nicky stuffed the memory down. She couldn't afford a panic attack, not now.

After what felt like an eternity of driving, the swampy road cleared onto a more open dirt road. The air was thick with wet soil and mud, like a bog. Scents of decay and rot coated the air. Nicky saw that if they went right, it would take them down another road that could lead back to the highway. Left, and they'd hit Sarah Mills's trailer within minutes.

Nicky looked at Ken, who was glancing around the forest. "I wanna get out of here too," Nicky said, "but we might as well finish this."

"You sure?"

"Yeah, let's go talk to her husband."

Ken nodded, but his expression was grim. Nicky had a bad feeling too. But their job wasn't to run when things got hard. It was to keep pushing forward until justice was served.

They were both silent as they drove down the road. Nicky was grateful, because she was tired of trying to talk through the tension.

They reached a fork in the road, and Nicky turned left. The GPS said she had one more turn to make, and then they'd be at the address.

"You see that?" Ken said, pointing out the windshield.

Nicky slowed the car down, trying to see what Ken was pointing at. Then she saw.

The old trailer sat perched on a small knoll, its walls tattered and stained. The roof was missing large chunks where a tree branch had smashed through it. The branches and leaves had tangled up in the broken window panes, obscuring the view inside. The surrounding trees created a natural canopy, shielding the trailer from the sun and the rain. The scent of rain and earth and wood was strong in the air.

Nicky drove the car up to the front door, which was hanging off its hinges.

She parked the car, and they both got out.

"Looks like nobody's been here for a while," Ken said.

Nicky sidled up to him. "Then let's be quiet, okay? The file said the husband still lives here."

"Right," he said, and drew his gun.

They went around back. Nicky saw a rickety old porch and a sliding screen door. A pair of muddy sneakers sat on the floor, and Nicky saw a can of beans sitting on a counter.

Ken pointed to the screen. "You think we should knock or...?"

Nicky nodded. They went out front and knocked on the old, falling apart door. But it just fell right open.

Nicky peered inside. If the outside of the trailer hadn't been unsettling, Nicky would have thought the inside would be in better condition. The living room was a mess: garbage and garbage bags and empty bottles were scattered around the room, and the wood floors were covered in dirt and dead bugs.

"There's no way someone lives here," Ken said.

"We saw the muddy boots," Nicky replied. "He lives here. Maybe he's just out."

Nicky thought on it. Maybe they should go inside. But that was the last place Nicky wanted to enter.

Suddenly, there was a loud noise, like glass shattering. They turned to see that one of the windows of the trailer had been shattered. Bits of glass littered the ground around it, and a jagged piece of the window frame was sticking out. The sound of shattering glass echoed through the forest, like a cry for help. It was like a death knell.

And from inside, the barrel of a shotgun pointed out.

Nicky didn't think--she just dove for cover.

CHAPTER THIRTEEN

A gunshot went off and resounded through the air, piercing Ken's ears.

He watched as Nicky's lithe frame expertly dodged out of the way. The shotgun blast went straight through the trailer's deck, sending wood flying everywhere. He knew, at that moment, this was about to get real.

Ken was at the side of the trailer now. With his gun pointed up, his heart pounding, he pressed his back to the wall. If he peeked too soon, he could get a shotgun blast to the face, and it'd be goodbye to his life. The idea of dying out here, in a horrible place like this, made his stomach roll. *Not gonna happen.*

He needed to stay calm. Be careful. Not get killed himself. And also not let his partner get killed.

In the corner of his eye, he saw Nicky rising from the ground. She had her gun out too. They exchanged a nod, and Nicky gestured to the back of the trailer.

"I can try to get in the back," she whispered, "if you can keep him distracted and get him talking."

Ken gave her another nod. It was a good enough plan, and he had experience talking psychos off ledges. With that, Nicky took off. Ken swallowed hard, then turned to where the shotgun was pointing.

"Hey, you in there!" His voice came out in a hoarse growl.

"What?" said a voice from inside the trailer. A small, angry, male voice.

"We're just here to talk, okay?" Ken said. "Why don't you put your weapon down and come out, and we can sort out our options here. How's that sound, bud? No need for anyone to get hurt."

There was a long pause. Somewhere in the forest, a bird squawked. "What are you doing here?" came the voice again. "This is private property."

"You're right. We're sorry to bother you," Ken said. "We just need to have a conversation, that's all, man."

"You bet you're sorry," came the voice. "I'm going to shoot you the second I see your face."

A bead of sweat ran down Ken's forehead and fell somewhere between his shoulder and his chest. "Just stay calm, please," Ken said. "Are you Derek Mills? We're with the FBI."

"Is that supposed to mean something to me?"

"It might. We're here about your wife."

Another pause. "Sarah? What about her?"

"She's missing," Ken said. "You know she's missing, don't you?"

"Yeah? Well guess what, I don't care."

"You don't care that your wife is missing?" Ken wasn't surprised, and he sure as hell wouldn't be surprised if this guy was the cause of Sarah's disappearance. Maybe the other girls' too. Hiding out here in the middle of the forest, shooting anyone who even comes near—this was a bad look for Derek Mills.

"Why would I care?" His voice had an odd, sing-song quality to it. "Sarah left me. Good riddance."

"Why did she leave you, Derek?"

Ken thought he heard a deranged giggle. "Because I'm so goddamn awesome. I'm so much better than her. I'm so much better than anybody."

"Did Sarah know that?"

"What are you, a goddamn therapist? What do you care, anyway?"

This guy was clearly unhinged. Ken needed to be careful—sometimes, nothing was more dangerous than a lunatic with a lethal weapon. He hoped Nicky knew what she was doing. They were way too far out to call for backup, and besides, the local PD here had already made it clear that they weren't too keen on helping the feds. Nicky and Ken were alone out here with this guy.

And Nicky had snuck from the back of the trailer to the front, but she wasn't in his line of sight anymore. She could easily get shot.

"Do you know where your wife is?" Ken asked. He had to keep him talking. If he could keep him talking, maybe he could keep him distracted. And maybe Nicky could slip in the back and get a better shot.

A pause. "Why should I tell you?"

"There might be hope for you yet. You can turn around and get help."

"You think I need your help?"

"No, I think you need help. And you should give yourself the chance to get it."

70

Derek laughed once. "That's not gonna work on me, agent or detective or whatever you are. Get off my property before I start shooting."

Nicky should have been in the trailer by now, but if she was, she was as silent as a mouse. Ken wanted to peek around the corner to see if Derek's shotgun was still pointing out the window, but it was risky. He decided to just keep talking.

"You must get pretty lonely out here all alone without your wife, Derek," Ken said.

"I don't even know what you're talking about," he said. "I'm not lonely. I've got friends."

"Who are your friends?"

"I'm not telling you that!"

"Derek, we're here to help you. And if you want us to, we can help you. If you just tell us what's going on, we can--"

"You're the ones who are going to be dead," Derek said. "I ain't going to jail. Over my dead body!"

Then, suddenly, Ken heard a click. The air went still. He wanted to call out for Nicky, to see where she was, but he wouldn't dare break the silence.

Then, he heard Nicky's voice: "Drop the weapon, Derek."

"Shit!" Derek yelled.

A gunshot went off.

Ken didn't think. He just ran right into the trailer. If Nicky got shot on the job, he'd never forgive himself. Maybe he hadn't always been her biggest fan--the woman could come across as too cocky and self-assured for her age, but since working closely with her, Ken had come to realize that there was a lot more to Nicky Lyons than her hardened exterior.

He wasn't about to let her die. Not on his watch.

Nicky was standing in the middle of the trailer, her gun pointed at Derek Mills. The barrel was smoking--and she had his shotgun in her hand.

Derek was on the ground, holding his arm. He was a scrawny-armed kid with bad tattoos and a rat tail. Blood leaked between his fingers. Clearly, Nicky had grazed him with the bullet, caused him to drop the weapon, and seized the shotgun.

Ken was impressed. He could see now why Nicky was considered the top agent in their office. She wasn't just competent--she was ballsy.

"You shot me!" Derek shouted, his voice shrill. "You can't do that! I'm an American! I have rights!"

"Put your hands behind your head, Derek," Nicky said. "And don't you dare move. You're under arrest."

"Oh yeah?" he said, still on the floor. "For what?"

This guy was a real piece of work. Ken leaned over him and grabbed him by the scruff of the neck, picking him up. "You did something to you wife, didn't you, Derek?" Ken said. "Tell me what you did to Sarah."

There was no way Derek would reasonably react the way he did and start shooting at federal agents if he were innocent. Clearly, he had something big to hide, and Ken was going to find out what.

Nicky came over, still holding her handgun. She'd thrown the shotgun off to the side, where Derek had no hope of reaching it.

"Walker, let's interrogate him on record, right here and now," Nicky said.

"I couldn't agree more." Ken dragged Derek to his feet, although his arm was still bleeding. He retched in pain. Ken threw Derek onto the couch, which was half-covered in garbage. Clearly, it'd been a long time since a woman had been in here. Based on Sarah's file, Ken didn't believe she would've lived like this, and he felt a pang of sadness for this missing girl and the messy life she'd left behind.

Nicky took out her phone and began recording. "This is Agent Nicky Lyons of the FBI, here with my partner, Agent Ken Walker, also of the FBI. We're here with one Derek Mills, age twenty-four."

Ken nodded at Nicky, then refocused on Derek. "Okay, Derek, tell us. What did you do to your wife, Sarah?"

"I didn't do anything," Derek said. "That bitch left me. I'm better off without her."

"But she was your wife, right? You two were married?" Ken said.

"Yeah, but she didn't deserve me. She didn't appreciate me."

"So you killed her?" Ken said.

Derek was shaking. "No! I didn't kill Sarah."

"Then where is she?" Nicky said. "Why can't we find her?"

"I don't know, okay? Maybe she's run off with someone else. Maybe she's dead. Maybe she's alive. What do I care? It's not like she ever loved me."

"That can't be true," Ken reasoned. "She married you, Derek. She must've loved you once. But maybe living out here took a toll on her. Did you kill her because she said she was gonna leave?"

Derek was quiet for several long moments. The trailer creaked around them as wind gusted outside, sending a warm breeze through the open windows that carried the scent of the woods. "I... I..." Derek broke down, running his hands over his eyes and through his hair. "Okay. Fine. I didn't mean to do it, okay? I didn't mean to kill her."

Ken's stomach dropped. Damn. He'd been hoping for a better outcome. But unfortunately, when a girl was missing for that long... this was almost always the true cause. Ken had seen too many violent husbands in his life, too many who'd gone too far, and it made him sick.

Nicky leaned in close. "What did you do, Derek?" she said. "Tell me what happened."

"Sarah... she was... she was so fucking perfect. I couldn't stand it. Such a know it all. Always saying how she could 'do better' than living out here with me. Well then why'd she even marry me, huh?"

"What did you do to her?" Nicky said, her expression hard. Ken wasn't in the mood for Derek's sob story either—he just wanted answers.

Derek broke down, sobbing. "I... I didn't mean to... but she's gone..."

Ken shook his head. He was disgusted by Derek. Sarah hadn't deserved that. Sarah was a good person who just wanted a better life—she didn't deserve to have that ripped away.

"I didn't mean to kill her!" Derek exclaimed. "But we were fighting, and she picked up my gun, and it just--it just went off."

Derek's voice was starting to break up. Ken wasn't sure he was able to understand everything he said.

"So, Derek, you killed your wife," Nicky said.

"She made me do it! She made me!" Derek said. "She had to pay. I didn't mean to hurt her. I didn't mean to kill her. But I did." Then, Derek started bawling uncontrollably again. "I killed my wife, okay? I did it."

Ken shook his head. This wasn't the kind of thing you could ever get used to.

Nicky leaned down. "Derek, you're going to go to jail for a long time," she said. "But we can help you, if you start talking to us. We can help you get some mental health care."

Derek screamed. "No! No! I don't need any help. I didn't do anything wrong. I didn't mean to kill Sarah."

"Where's the body?" Nicky said.

Being asked point blank seemed to make Derek sweat. His eyes were darting all over the place, like he'd been backed into a corner and he knew it. Finally, he said, "I, it's..."

"Derek," Nicky warned. "It's over. Tell us where Sarah is so we can bring her home."

"I dumped it in the woods. I didn't know what else to do."

Jesus, Ken thought. It was so cold, so evil. To kill the woman who'd married you and just leave her body out there in the woods for the animals to feast on.

"Did you kill anyone else?" Ken asked.

"No!" Derek cried. "I would never have done that. I didn't mean to kill Sarah. I loved her. I really, really did. I loved her."

There was a change in Derek's demeanor. His eyes narrowed, and he looked at Ken. "I bet you think I'm shitty, huh? You think I'm a loser because I didn't appreciate Sarah. Well, you should never treat your wife like shit. You should appreciate her every day. She's the most important person in your life, so you should treat her that way."

Silence. This guy was beyond crazy, and Ken didn't know what to think about him. He definitely belonged behind bars, that was for sure. But if he killed Sarah, did he also kill Meghan Salinger? There would be a motive for Sarah--but there didn't seem to be anything linking Derek to Meghan.

Nicky must've been thinking the same thing, because on her phone, she pulled up a photo of Meghan Salinger and shoved it in Derek's face.

"Do you recognize this woman?" Nicky demanded.

Derek looked at her and scowled. "What? No!"

"You sure about that?" Nicky said. "Because she looks pretty familiar to me."

"That's not Sarah," Derek said. "That's not my wife. I would know. That girl looks different."

"You're right, she's not your wife," Nicky said. "This is another woman who went missing. And I think you know something about it."

"I don't know anything about that girl," Derek said. "I haven't seen her. I have no idea what you're talking about."

"Don't play dumb with us, Derek," Nicky said, "because we're going to figure out what's going on, just like we did with Sarah."

"I'm telling you," Derek pleaded, "I killed Sarah by accident, but I don't know who that other chick is!"

Ken didn't know what to think. All he knew was that if he was being honest with himself, he felt like Derek was actually telling the truth on this one. Ken didn't think that Derek was the guy who killed Meghan Salinger. There was just no connection between them, and it'd make no sense.

Either way, they needed to take him in.

74

Nicky slapped cuffs on Derek. "Derek Mills, you're under arrest for the murder of Sarah Mills..."

"NO!" Derek yelled. "NO! That's not what happened! I just said that! I didn't mean to kill Sarah! She made me do it! She made me, okay? She made me! Fucking bitch--and now she's dead. I can't believe I did that. It's all her fault! I hate her! I hate her! I wish she was still around, so I could kill her all over again!"

"Jesus, Derek," Nicky said.

Ken couldn't believe what he was seeing. This guy was a monster. He was a psychopath.

And now, he was going to jail for it.

Ken took a deep breath. He had nothing to complain about—this was a job well done. He just hoped he could figure out what happened to Meghan Salinger before she met the same fate as Sarah.

CHAPTER FOURTEEN

Another dead end.

Nicky walked into the motel room and heaved out a sigh. Ken was close behind her, but they'd been quiet since they left the Frankstown precinct, where Derek Mills was being detained. Nicky didn't trust the cops there to do their job right, so she'd called in a favor from the FBI-- a Hollywood, Florida, detective would be coming to take Derek into his custody, where he'd get the proper treatment that he deserved: a trial and definitely jail time. The recorded confession was more than enough to prove Derek had killed Sarah.

But then there was the question of Meghan.

As far as Nicky could see, there was no connection between Derek and Meghan, and no reason for him to have had anything to do with Meghan's disappearance at all. Nicky was more than happy to get another dirtbag off the streets, but as for her case... it was another dead end.

Nicky slapped a stack of folders on the table in the motel room and sat down, with Ken sitting next to her. She figured their best bet was to go over other recent cases and see if they could find any connection. The folders were neatly organized and had been stacked in order. There was a photograph of a woman and a child inside the first folder. The woman had long, red hair and the child had bright blue eyes. The photograph was taken at a park, and the child was smiling. There was a note attached to the photograph. It said, *"My beautiful daughter. I miss her so much."*

Another victim. This one, a young mother. Nicky sighed. She'd already reviewed these files. But maybe they'd missed something the first time. Maybe they'd overlooked a potential suspect. Maybe they'd overlooked something that connected Meghan to someone else.

All they had to do was look at the files, and they'd know. The answer was in there. Nicky just needed to find it.

The files were all missing girls' cases from the last three years. All of them unsolved. Some of them were still being investigated, but so far, nothing had been found.

The first one was a sixteen-year-old who'd gone missing outside of Hollywood, Florida. The second one was a high school student who'd gone missing in the countryside. The third one was an eighteen-year-old who'd disappeared from soccer practice.

Nicky sighed. This was a dead end. Just like everything else. The stuff she'd found out about Derek was irrelevant--it had nothing to do with Meghan.

But that was just it, wasn't it? The cops had screwed up the other case by assuming Meghan Salinger's case was connected to Sarah Mills's, and then they stopped looking into Sarah at all--not realizing that the very person who'd killed her was her own husband. And he wasn't exactly subtle.

It was all dirty police work, and it made Nicky sick. This was part of why she'd joined the FBI. She'd always felt like if she wanted to do something right, she had to do it herself. Rosie's case had gone cold before Nicky graduated from the FBI academy, but she'd always hoped to reopen it officially herself and get the job done. However, it wasn't that simple; she had obvious personal investments in the case, which had made it so her superiors always said no. Nicky was needed on other cases, open cases, and the case of Rosie Lyons was long declared dead.

She glanced over the file in front of her. But she couldn't stop herself from going back in time. Driving through the woods today had brought her back to all those years ago. The terrain was very different--a Florida forest looks a lot different from a West Virginia one. But still.

Nicky could see Rosie again, running through the forest, her long hair flying around her. The leaves, the sky, the trees, the dirt... the colors were different, but the scene was the same.

She closed her eyes and went back to that night, all those years ago. Sometimes, reliving it was almost an addiction.

After the man who'd abducted them had thrown them in the lake, Nicky was certain her life--and Rosie's--was about to end. She'd never forget the feeling of her lungs growing tighter as her body begged her to breathe, but if she took in a breath, she'd fill her lungs with lake water.

But then--something cut her hands free. She kicked as hard as she could and swam to the surface. She rose above the water and gasped for air, greeted by the starry night sky. And moments later, Rosie came up, gasping, too.

There was a moment of relief before the fear set back in.

The man came up too, holding a knife.

He had freed them.

Soaking wet, with his clothes stuck to his skinny, bony frame, the man wandered back to the shore as Nicky and Rosie stayed there, petrified. The gun was in his belt, and he sheathed the knife. He turned to them with a smile as they floated in the lake, confused.

"That's how easy it can all go away," he said, smiling.

They could see his face in the moonlight now. It was crooked, his nose long and oblong. And his eyes--they had no soul.

"Let this be a lesson," he said, amused. "I own your lives now. I can take them away whenever I please. If you do as I say, this will go easier for you. Now, get out of the water."

They'd had no choice but to obey.

"Lyons?" Ken's voice pulled Nicky from her reverie.

Her eyes snapped to him. He was across the table from her in the motel, frowning, his loose-fitting shirt partially unbuttoned. His eyes were intense and bore into her.

"You good?" he asked.

Nicky shifted away. It was uncomfortable to know that Ken was starting to know her enough to recognize when she was in another world.

"Yeah, I'm fine," she lied.

"What were you thinking about?" he asked.

"Nothing," she answered quickly. But then she sighed, reminding herself of her whole "honesty" policy as a leader. "Just... my sister again. I'd really rather not talk about it." She shook her head. "I'd rather focus on our current case. We're gonna go over everything again, okay?"

Ken nodded. "We'll find her."

Nicky tried to smile. "Yeah, we will. You see anything relevant?"

Ken let out a sigh as he flipped through a file. "Not really. I don't see how these cases could be connected."

"No, me neither," Nicky said. "But we have to cover all our bases. Let me go through these again. Maybe I'll find something we missed."

Refocusing on the file, Nicky took aim at the missing persons cases. All girls like Rosie, all gone without a trace.

The first was a girl who'd been abducted by her mother's drug dealer. They hadn't had contact with each other since the girl was young, and the mother didn't even know if her daughter was still alive.

The second girl went missing after a car crash. Her parents thought she was dead.

The third was a woman who was in a coma after surgery. A mix-up happened, and she was given somebody else's medication. Chances were that these cases were as unrelated to Meghan Salinger as Sarah Mills's case.

She flipped through the file, studying each photo closely. In each one, the missing girl looked happy and carefree.

It was such a contrast to Rosie's face as she was taken away.

Something nagged at Nicky. She flipped back to the first page of the file and skimmed it quickly.

It was strange--the more she read, the further away she got from Rosie. She tried to force herself to come back and study Rosie's photo again, to think about what might have happened to her.

But there was something about the case--something familiar...

A name jumped out at her.

Ella White.

And right next to the name on the file was the word SOLVED.

"What the hell?" Nicky said. "This one actually was solved."

"Really?" Ken asked. *"Actually* solved? Or 'solved' by the Frankstown police's standards?"

Nicky flipped Ella's file open. She was another redhead, like Meghan and Sarah. Nicky eagerly read through the words on the file until she reached the conclusion.

Her heart fell to the floor.

"She was found dead," Nicky whispered.

"What? Where?"

Nicky read each word on the file carefully. Ella had been missing for six months before she was found dead. And she was discovered in an abandoned warehouse of a now-defunct company called Home Furniture.

Nicky paused. Home Furniture. Why did that feel so... familiar?

She thought back to yesterday, in the prison. Bernard Brown and his empty, soulless eyes. The words he'd said to Nicky. *"All roads lead to home."*

"Shit," Nicky said aloud. If Brown somehow knew something, then this could be the clue they'd needed. "She was found in an old warehouse," Nicky said. "But Ken, it's called Home Furniture. You remember what Brown said at the prison."

His dark brow furrowed, blue eyes hidden beneath long, inky eyelashes. "Yeah, a bunch of psychotic shit."

"All roads lead to home," Nicky told him.

Ken leaned back in the chair. "You think Brown knew about the warehouse?"

"Maybe," Nicky said. She looked back down at the file. "According to this, no one else was discovered at the warehouse, but we've got a lot of missing girls on our hands here, all from the same area."

"And from the same time period," Ken added.

Nicky nodded. "Yeah. All those girls went missing within the last three years, under similar circumstances. But Ella is the only one who turned up dead...?"

"This definitely stinks," Ken agreed.

Nicky's mind raced. She looked over the report of the search of the warehouse. It said they never found any other bodies there, and that the place had been searched thoroughly. But maybe they missed something. The police here hadn't proved their commitment to the cause.

Was it possible? She couldn't quite wrap her head around it. The idea that there could be more girls at the warehouse... Nicky wasn't sure if that was something she even wanted to find. But at the same time, this was her job, and if she wanted any hope in hell of finding Meghan, then she had to chase down every lead, no matter how slim.

"We need to check this out," she told Ken.

He nodded. "Yeah, I think we do."

Nicky looked down at Ella's file. "It's not far from here," she said. "It's off the highway, but we can make it there fast with me driving."

They ripped outside of the motel room. Maybe with this one, they would finally get some answers.

CHAPTER FIFTEEN

Nicky pressed her foot to the gas, zipping the car down the highway as Ken sat in the passenger seat. She didn't know what they were going to find at this warehouse, but her palms were sweaty with anticipation--and fear.

Anticipation that they could make a break in the case.

Fear of what the price of that break might be.

She didn't know what they'd find there. But she had a gut feeling it wasn't going to be pretty. Nicky knew the police had already searched the place when they found Ella's body, but she didn't trust that they'd done a thorough enough job. There was more to this story—Nicky could feel it in her gut.

Nicky turned off the highway onto a thin, cracked road, through a forest. At least this one wasn't a swamp. Still, she had to avoid potholes left, right, and center. The last thing they needed to deal with was a busted wheel in the middle of nowhere.

At long last, the warehouse appeared through the trees up ahead. It was surrounded by a tall fence with only one way in and out--a large metal gate. On the other side, a green sign with white lettering directed them to Home Furniture.

The trees around the warehouse were bare, the leaves crispy brown on the ground. As they pulled up, Nicky saw weeds and brush growing around the steps leading to the door.

"Wow," Nicky said. "This place hasn't operated in years."

"Could be squatters," Ken warned.

"All the way out here, I doubt it," Nicky said. "But we should be prepared."

"And if anything stinks like black mold or asbestos, we might have no choice but to call backup," Ken said.

"Yeah," Nicky muttered, "but I'd rather see what we're dealing with ourselves before we get any more hands involved."

Nicky parked out front of the gate. They got out of the car and walked up to the metal fence. Police tape fluttered from the fence. There were a few mismatched pieces of furniture stacked near the entrance of the warehouse, old and decaying, likely filled with bugs.

Nicky pushed her way through the front gate and let Ken through. She shut it behind them.

"So, what's our plan, Agent Lyons?" Ken asked.

Nicky looked around. "Well, it seems pretty abandoned. I want to see if there's any way in behind all this."

Ken nodded. "Got it." He headed around back, and Nicky followed, but there was no way to get into the warehouse without smashing in the back door. "It looks like there could be a way in over here."

Ken led them around the back, where a broken window gave them easy access.

"Great," Nicky said. "Let's try and be as quiet as possible. I don't know if anyone's in there, but we should assume they're close by."

Nicky took the lead, and Ken followed as she crept into the dark warehouse.

When Nicky had seen the pictures of this place in the file, it hadn't seemed like anything special. Now, as she stood in the center of the open space, she was awestruck. The warehouse was so much bigger than it had seemed on the outside. The warehouse was dark inside, with only a few rays of sunlight shining through the cracks in the windows. It was quiet, too, except for the distant sound of birds chirping outside the walls.

And the smell. It was awful.

The smell of rot and decay filled the room. It was a nauseating mixture of mold and dead animal. The stench was so bad that it would make even the strongest person gag. The furniture was splintered and disintegrating, and the walls were peeling and covered in graffiti.

"Nicky, wait," Ken said suddenly.

Nicky turned to him. "What is it?"

Ken was holding his hand up, a silencing gesture. He slowly walked toward the back, where Nicky saw a crack in the wall that led into another room.

"What is it?" Nicky asked softly.

Ken pointed to the room. "I think I heard something. I'm going to check it out."

Nicky watched as Ken tiptoed carefully into the room. She held her breath, listening for any sound, but she didn't hear anything. Ken slowly turned back to her and made the okay sign.

Nicky felt her shoulders relax.

Ken motioned for her to come.

Quietly, Nicky crept toward the room. She peered around Ken to see what was inside. There was a long table. It looked like an office room of some kind, with some old desks sitting around with clutter still everywhere: pencils, dirty papers, even a couple of textbooks.

Nicky moved toward a desk, and Ken did the same, going across the room to see if there was anything valuable.

Nicky didn't see anything of interest on her desk, though. She was just about to turn away when she saw something out of the corner of her eye.

Poking out of one of the drawers was a roll of paper. Nicky frowned and opened the drawer, then pulled it out. She rolled out the paper.

It was a blueprint of the factory. The old blueprint was a faded cream color, with thick black lines crisscrossing the page. There were a few discolored spots. The writing was in faded ink, though still legible. But it was clear enough to understand the building's layout.

"Walker, check this out," Nicky said to Ken. He came over and peered over Nicky's shoulder.

Ken looked at the blueprint and back at the room. "That makes sense. This property was a furniture factory before the owner went bankrupt and disappeared."

"Yes, but this says the factory was renovated in 2004," Nicky said, pointing at the writing. "This is the original blueprint."

Nicky had brought her handbag with her with Ella White's case file in it. She pulled it out and read it over.

According to the report, the police scoured the building for anything else, but Ella's body was the only one found.

They had checked all the rooms on the main floor, and the upper level, including all the bathrooms.

Nicky looked back at the blueprint and frowned. Wait... there was something missing.

"Ken, this place used to have a basement. There's nothing in the report about it."

Ken squinted at the blueprint. "It does look like you could go down to something here."

Nicky pointed to the spot where the basement used to be. She looked at the report, then back at the blueprint. She really didn't know what to think of this.

"Do you think it's possible...?" Nicky began.

"That it's still down there? Of course. We need to check it out."

The map was pretty large, so they positioned it in the middle, on a table. The light from the windows spilled onto the paper, making the lines and writing easier to see.

83

Nicky pointed at the diagram on the map. "Okay, so according to this, the entrance to the basement used to be here."

They took the map and walked out into the main area. Nicky ignored the stagnant smell as she made her way toward a wall, way on the far side of the building. Sure enough, there was a door there. Nicky exchanged a look with Ken before she opened it.

Only they didn't see any stairs leading down to a basement.

It was just a storage closet, equipped with an old broom. That smell, though, like something rotting, became stronger.

"The blueprint said it should be in here," Nicky said.

"Hold on." Ken shimmied past Nicky, into the closet. He started knocking on the walls, starting with the right one. It made a hard sound as his knuckle clacked against it. "Concrete," he said to himself. Nicky stood back and watched.

Then, on the back wall, the sound became more hollow.

Ken looked back at Nicky. "Drywall."

Nicky's heart rate picked up. This was it. They must have put the drywall up to conceal the basement. But if it was just drywall, then--

"We need to break it down," Nicky said. She looked over her shoulder, into the warehouse. This place was huge. It had to have some tools around.

Then, Nicky saw it: across the room, embedded into the wall, was a glass box. It contained a fire extinguisher.

This would have to do.

"Hold on," Nicky said to Ken. She dashed across the warehouse, broke into the box, and took out the fire extinguisher. Ken was standing there with his arms crossed when she came back, fire extinguisher in hand.

"Stay back, Walker," she said.

Ken laughed and shook his head, then stepped away. "You sure you don't want me to handle that?"

"I've got it," Nicky said. Then she smashed it into the wall.

The fire extinguisher made a loud noise as it slammed into the wall. It also left a sizable dent. But no drywall broke away, no entrance. Nicky hit it again. This time, the drywall cracked, then broke apart. Nicky looked at the wall, then took a step back and hit it again. And again.

The cracks spread, and the wall became more porous. Eventually, a dark gap appeared.

And with it, the most pungent stench Nicky had ever smelled.

She immediately covered her nose with her shirt. "What the hell?"

It was like rotten eggs mixed with a dumpster that had been simmering in the sun. Ken pulled his shirt over his nose too. Nicky kept on hitting the drywall, over and over again, until she created a gap big enough for them to squeeze through.

Ken, still covering his nose, came over with a flashlight. They peeked inside the hole.

And there were the stairs. Old, metal, rusty stairs.

"Jesus," Ken said. "There's definitely something dead down there. We should call backup."

"They'll take forever to get here," Nicky said. "Let's check first."

She couldn't walk away without finding out. She had to know.

It looked like it was a standard old basement, with stone walls and wooden floor. It was damp, with reservoirs of water on the ground. Cobwebs stretched across the ceiling.

It was a mess. But it was nothing terrifying, at least on the surface.

"I don't know what's causing this smell, but it's unreal," Ken said as he shined his flashlight around the room.

"I know," Nicky said. "Whatever's causing that can't be good."

As they were making their way through the dark, dank basement, Nicky noticed the old furnace. She frowned and went up to it. Beneath the putrid smell, it also smelled like soot.

Had somebody used this thing recently?

"Lyons," Ken suddenly said with urgency in his voice.

Nicky looked across the room, where he was pointing to a door. "Smell's really strong over here."

Nicky swallowed, hard, before she stormed over. "Looks like we're in the right place then."

She tried the handle, but it was locked. She kicked it, but nothing. "We need to open this."

"Take the flashlight," Ken said, then he put it in her hands and began pacing around.

Nicky stood there, holding the flashlight with shaking hands. She hated this. She hated the fact that she could hear her heart beating in her chest.

Just breathe. This is what you're here for.

She took a deep breath as Ken approached the door. He stopped and kicked it, this time with more force.

The door burst open.

And the smell came in full force.

Nicky shone the flashlight in, squinting. The smell was so strong it even stung her eyes.

She peered into the light.

And inside the room was a pile of dead women, each at varying stages of decay.

But Nicky immediately recognized one of the women in the pile, who was less decayed than the others beneath her. This was one of the girls from the files.

Nicky's stomach rolled. She fell back, but Ken caught her. Her head spun so violently she thought she might drop dead right then and there.

This wasn't just a kidnapper.

This was a serial killer.

And right now, he had another victim.

CHAPTER SIXTEEN

His knuckles were turning white against the steering wheel as he gripped it hard, wishing it was her neck.

She'd ruined everything. Messed it all up. All that planning, all the work he'd put into their big wedding day--it was all for nothing. How could he waste so much time on such an unworthy hag?

As he erratically drove, he could hear her screaming in the trunk. "Help! Help me!"

At the next red light, he intentionally slammed hard on his brakes to shut her up. When he heard her thud against the car, he smiled. A moment of happiness in his rage.

Stupid "bride." She didn't even deserve to wear that wedding dress. He hated that it was still on her body, but it wouldn't be for long--he was going to rid her of it.

Her vows had been awful. No creativity, not even a mention of how wonderful he was. All she'd done was try to manipulate him.

"Please, if I marry you, will you let me go? I'll still come see you, but I need to have space..." That was what she'd said, and it was despicable.

He mocked her out loud and made a face. "Please let me go, please let me go."

She was not his true love and she never would be.

So, he needed to find another.

And he had just the right girl in mind.

As he drove up the street, he saw the diner up ahead. Finally, relief. His true love was in there. In the trunk, his fiancé kicked and screamed.

"Help me! Somebody! Help me!"

He shook his head. "That's not going to do you any good, bride."

He parked his car in the parking lot at the back of the diner. Through the window of the diner, he could see her: his true love, waiting tables, wearing her uniform. Once she was with him, she'd never have to work a day in her life again. She was perfect. She was the one.

"She'd actually appreciate me," he said to his now *ex*-fiancé. "You were a waste. A waste of resources."

87

"Let me go!" her muffled voice yelled, barely audible. He needed to shut her up—she would give them both away. Sighing, he got out of the car and went to the trunk, opening it. His ex was tied up, and she went to scream—but swiftly, he brought his fist down on her face, shutting her up and giving her a bloody nose. She was quiet after that.

He went to the front of the car and sat on the hood.

Soon, his true love would be going on her break. She would leave through the back door, and that was when he would strike.

As she got up from the table, his true love's eyes met his in the window.

She was watching.

She was waiting for him.

He cried out in joy.

He'd found her. It was predestined.

They recognized each other, and now there was no need for him to go through with his plan with the other girl. He'd just come up with a new plan, and it was better than the old one.

He leaned back on the trunk, waiting for his true love to come out. The sky was a beautiful blue, with fluffy white clouds. The sun shone brightly, and there was a gentle breeze that rustled the leaves and flowers. It was a perfect day.

His true love finally came out through the back door. He waved at her, smiling ear-to-ear. She looked over her shoulder with a look of confusion on her face, then slowly approached.

"Hello there," he said.

She frowned, perplexed. "Do I know you?"

"Oh, of course!" He stood up straight, then squinted at her. "Oh, my, I'm sorry. I thought you were someone else!"

"Oh..." She laughed awkwardly, leaning away.

"Would you mind helping me with something real quick?" he asked. Still smiling wide, to show he meant no harm. He'd never hurt his one true love.

He just needed to get her in his car.

"I've dropped my glasses under my seat and I just can't reach them," he said. "You have a small arm. Think you could help me out?"

She nodded, unsure. "Are they important? Like, can't see without--"

"They're important," he said, irritated. "They're really important."

He got frustrated waiting for her to come to the car. He sighed, looking at the window. She was still hesitating. Why would she hesitate on their love? *Come here, my sweet, come here...*

He was really hoping she'd be nice enough to help.

"I don't think that's a good idea." She started to walk away.

"Come on! I can't see! I need to get to the eye doctor after work to get my prescription changed and I can't see without them."

He looked at her, desperate.

"Well, alright," she sighed.

He breathed a sigh of relief. "Great!" He got back into the car and pulled his seat forward so she could climb in. He pretended to look for his glasses, even though he knew they were in the glove compartment.

He smiled.

Now was his time to strike. Now, she'd be his true love forever

Out with the old, in with the new.

CHAPTER SEVENTEEN

Back at the motel room, Nicky typed diligently on her laptop--there had to be someone out there who had access to or knew about the warehouse, with a criminal history. Somewhere to at least start pointing the finger at whoever could've done this.

Ken was across from her, reviewing files for something, anything.

But they'd both been quiet for a while. After the discovery they'd made in the warehouse, the chances of Meghan Salinger being found alive were slim.

And they were both thinking it.

The FBI had swept onto the scene upon Nicky and Ken's call--some agents even came in on helicopters to get an eye on what they'd found. It was far from pretty. Now, they were working to clean the mess up, and had already identified a handful of the victims. Each time a victim was identified, Nicky got an alert on her phone. All of them had been girls who'd gone missing in surrounding areas in the past seven or so months. Just like Meghan.

Nicky was thankful that she and Ken had been able to take off to keep chasing leads, because the smell of that factory was burned into Nicky's brain. She'd never forget the stench. And she'd never forget the dead faces of those women.

She had to find who did this and make them pay.

The room was quiet, save the sound of typing. She was trying to get to the bottom of this. She was trying to get Meghan back.

She was trying to stay sane.

At least they had something to do.

Then, suddenly, a phone call. Nicky picked it up.

Frankstown police station. What the...?

"This is Agent Lyons," she said, exchanging a look with Ken.

"Agent Lyons, hello. This is Sheriff Corbin."

"Sheriff..." Nicky trailed off, surprised he was calling her. "I'm sure you've heard what we found. The case is officially being handled by the FBI."

"I know. But we just got a call in, and I wanted to tell you first."

Nicky's breath caught. Maybe there was a good bone in Sheriff Corbin's body.

"Another woman went missing, pretty similar situation to the others. Young, under twenty-five, vanished without a trace from her job. Name's Lauren Klein."

Nicky's head spun. "Are you sure?"

"Yeah. Don't know if it's related yet. But with what you found earlier... I figured you should know right away."

"Thank you. Please forward the details to me."

"Will do."

Nicky hung up. Ken was looking at her, frowning. "What's that about?"

"A woman went missing from her job. The sheriff said it was 'pretty similar' to the other victims."

"Christ." Ken set his papers aside. "I don't know if I can handle another one."

Nicky swallowed. This was much worse than she realized because an awareness came over her.

All of those girls were at different stages of decay. The one on top, who Nicky had recognized from the files, was by far the most recent. In fact, she was hardly decayed at all.

Her heart began to pound. "Ken," she said, "Meghan could still be alive. But she won't be for long."

"What makes you say that?"

"The others were all in different stages of decay. But I recognized the girl. She was at the top of the pile. She was the most recent victim. If Meghan is still alive, she's probably the next one on the pile." Nicky paused. "Walker, I think that he's been exchanging his victims. Once he's done with one, he murders them and gets another."

"Jesus," Ken said. "Looks like we've got a psycho who's gone on a killing spree, he's been getting away with it, and he's not going to stop until he's caught."

"Exactly. But if we want any hope of saving Meghan Salinger, we have to find a lead, now."

"I'm trying over here," Ken said. "Did you find anything at all?"

Nicky refocused on her laptop. No, she hadn't found anything, not yet. But she'd been on to something before the call. The warehouse was pretty obscure and wouldn't be known to the average person. She'd requested a list of previous employees, but had yet to get it.

Bernard Brown's warning flickered back into Nicky's mind.

"All roads lead to home..."

Home...

She couldn't stop thinking about it, or that one word. 'Home.'

She opened up her internet browser and frowned at the screen.

Employees weren't the only ones who would know about the warehouse. There could be construction workers.

Or a real estate agent.

Someone who sells 'homes.'

At some point, somebody would have had to represent the warehouse, right? It had to have a realtor at some point in its life.

Maybe it was a shot in the dark, but Nicky's hunch had been right before--it had led them to the warehouse.

But there was one person who could dig up dirt way faster than she could, so she took out her phone and called Grace. Grace eagerly picked up.

"Agent Lyons!" she exclaimed. "I've been waiting to hear from you. I heard about the warehouse. It's so awful."

"I know, Grace," Nicky said. Across from her, Ken watched curiously, listening, so Nicky put the phone on speaker. "We can talk about it later. I need you to help me dig up dirt on the warehouse. Did they try to sell it when the company went bankrupt? As in, was there ever a realtor attached to it?"

"One second," Grace said. On the other end, Nicky heard a keyboard clacking. A moment later, Grace came back on the line. "I have the name of the realtor. His name is Jordan Katz."

Nicky's heart skipped a beat. "Katz," she said. "What's his story?"

Grace let out a whistle. "Not super pretty. He's been accused of sexually assaulting more than a few girls. Nothing ever made it through court, but we both know that doesn't mean it never happened."

Nicky gritted her teeth. This could be their guy. But the assault accusations alone weren't enough to prove he was a serial killer.

"I need to know more," Nicky said. "I need you to give me every bit of dirt on this guy."

"Okay, I'm looking now. Stay on the line. Let's see what else Jordan Katz has in his closet..."

With bated breath, Nicky waited for Grace to tell her more.

With a hard look in her eyes, she stared at the pile of files in front of her.

"Here we go," Grace said. "Okay, I've got a few things. Jordan Katz is thirty-seven-years-old now. He grew up in a pretty poor family. He was always kind of a leech and had his first assault accusation back in high school. But he was smart, and he managed to get a full-ride to a prestigious university, and then went to law school where he was accused of assaulting more girls. They dropped charges, but he blew his career out of the water on that one. So, he ended up as a real estate agent. And a successful one at that."

"Sounds like a great guy," Nicky muttered.

"He's also into dating apps. Like, serially."

Nicky squared her shoulders, looked Ken in the eyes, who was still watching and listening intently.

"How serially are we talking?" Nicky asked.

On the other side of the phone, Nicky heard more typing. "I'm into his personal bubble now. He's been accused of catfishing girls. Mostly in Frankstown and surrounding areas. Even some in Hollywood, Florida."

"Catfishing how?" Nicky asked.

"Well, for one, his dating profile, according to this database, lists him as thirty-three. And that picture does not look like his mugshot, I'll tell you that. And wait, hold on..."

"What is it?" Nicky's heart was in her throat.

"Holy moly," Grace said. "Lyons, you're not going to believe this, but it looks like Katz actually matched on a dating app with Meghan Salinger."

The ball had dropped. Nicky and Ken looked at each other in panic.

"Are you sure?" Nicky asked.

"Positive. I'm on a social media thread right now. Some girls are publicly talking about getting played and catfished by Katz. And Meghan commented. It's her profile, and it happened before she went missing."

Nicky didn't know how a brain like Grace's worked to pick up on all this stuff so fast, but she was impressed, to say the least.

"Got it, Grace. You're amazing. I just need one more thing." Nicky paused. "Text me both his personal and work addresses."

"Can do," Grace said. "Be careful. Both of you."

"We will."

With that, Nicky hung up, immediately rising to her feet. Within seconds, her phone buzzed--the text from Grace. Perfect.

Now, Nicky knew exactly where to find this son of a bitch and bring him down.

CHAPTER EIGHTEEN

Evening painted the sky as Nicky rushed into the realtor's office, which was shockingly ritzy. The office was modern and crisp, outfitted in the latest styles and newest tech. Everything was high-end and sleek. The furniture was leather, and Nicky could tell from the smell that it was real.

Apparently, this Katz guy was no low baller, despite the fact that he never sold that old warehouse. A perky young receptionist sat behind a sleek desk, fingers clacking away at a keyboard, when Nicky and Ken stormed up.

"Can I help you?" she asked, standing at attention, but all Nicky did was hold up her badge.

"I'm looking for Jordan Katz."

"Mr. Katz isn't here right now," she said. "Can I deliver a message?"

No. Nicky wouldn't accept that. She needed Katz now. If anyone had something to do with those girls dying, it had to be him. It was too much of a coincidence for him to not only have a history of assaulting women, but for him to have also matched with Meghan on a dating app.

Katz had guilty written all over him.

"A message isn't good enough," Nicky said. She held her badge up higher. "We're with the FBI. We need to know where Katz went."

"Um, well--"

Nicky didn't like using intimidation when she didn't need to, but in this case, she did need to. Meghan's life was on the line.

Nicky couldn't lose another.

She couldn't lose Rosie again.

"If you know where he is," Nicky said, "you need to tell us. It would be an obstruction of justice not to."

"I--" The receptionist looked between the pair of them, chest trembling with uncertainty. Nicky did feel bad. This girl probably had an allegiance to Katz, for whatever reason, but Nicky had to do her job.

"You're doing the right thing," Nicky said. "Please. You need to tell us."

With that, the receptionist swallowed and nodded. She picked up a pen and scribbled down an address, then handed it to Nicky, who took it instantly.

"He's throwing a banquet at a theater nearby," she said. "It's sort of an invite-only, black-tie event. Only Mr. Katz's top clients and family members are invited. I think it's for his uncle's retirement or something. Really, that's all I know."

"Thanks." Nicky didn't waste a second, turning on her foot and hurrying out of the office with Ken right on her tail. They could take this bastard down. It was time.

"Gonna let me drive for once?" Ken asked as they hurried up to the car.

"Not a chance," Nicky said. She was in charge of this mission, so she liked being in charge of the wheels.

The sun was setting, casting an orange hue over the parking lot. The parking lot was still warm from the sun, but the air was cool, the asphalt hot. Nicky slid into the driver's seat. The moment Ken got in the passenger side and strapped in, Nicky pressed her foot to the gas.

If Katz really was the killer, and he was busy at some event, then there was a chance Meghan was still alive. Nicky wasn't too late.

Too late, like she'd been too late all those years ago, with Rosie. No matter what Nicky was doing, it always came back to this. As Nicky drove, she couldn't help but return to that night all those years ago. Maybe what Meghan had gone through--or was currently going through--was the same. Maybe she felt the same fear, the same terror.

After the man had thrown Nicky and Rosie into the lake, only to pull them out, he took them into what would be their prison for the next several days.

The cabin. It was dark, dank, and smelled of mildew and mold. They thought for sure he would kill them. Nicky would never forget the way she and Rosie clung to each other on the cabin floor, terrified of what was to come next. She could never forget the way the building creaked around them, and how every moment spent in it had been terrifying.

The first night there, they didn't sleep at all—how could they? With every creak in the house, they were waiting for the man to come back, to kill them finally. But it never happened. They lived through, until the sun began to rise through the narrow gaps in the building's walls.

That would only be the beginning of their torment.

That was why Nicky had to save Meghan before it was too late. If she was alive, she deserved to get out of her hell, the same way Nicky had.

***

The car screeched to a halt in front of the opulent theater. It stood grand and white against the dark night sky. Nicky parked and quickly hurried out with Ken.

They barely managed to make it to the doors before they were swarmed with security--who were actual police officers in uniform.

"Excuse me!" one guy said. "This is a private event. I'm gonna have to ask you to leave."

Nicky and Ken whipped out their badges. "FBI," Nicky said. "We need through. Now."

The cops exchanged glances. "We can't do that," the one guy, a scrawny officer with a goatee, said.

Nicky struggled to keep her cool. "You can, and you will. This is a federal investigation."

"You can either let us through," Ken said, "or you can deal with the fact that you're going to be personally responsible for allowing a murderer to go free."

"Murderer?" The cop scowled. "What are you talking about? This is a very influential crowd. You two are in the wrong place."

"We're in the right place," Nicky said. "Trust me on that. We need to get in there. Now."

The officer looked more nervous than before, shifting from one foot to the other. "This is a private event," he said. "Unless you have a warrant, I can't let you in there."

Nicky glanced at Ken. The man was taking in the entire situation. He was thinking quickly, just as Nicky was.

"I'm not saying we have a warrant, but we do have probable cause. This is a federal investigation, and you will be personally responsible if we don't get to go through," Ken said.

"That's right," Nicky said. "We're going through, and we're going through right now. So either let us, or you're going to be in deep shit. Is it really worth it?"

The officer's jaw clenched, but once he looked at the other officers who were joining the conversation, he must have realized that he didn't have a choice.

"No," one of the other cops said. "We should call this in, get a warrant."

"I'm not making the call," the officer said. "I'm not risking my job over this. Those are federal agents."

The man Nicky and Ken had first spoken to didn't look pleased. "Fine, but if you screw up, I'm holding you personally responsible."

"I've got this," the first officer said, and with that, Nicky and Ken were rushed into the theater. Nicky entered the lobby and instantly her gaze zeroed in on the stage just ahead.

She hadn't realized it before, but the place was already full of people. Everyone was dressed to the nines in fancy gowns and tuxedos, sipping on glasses of champagne while they chatted. No one even gave Nicky and Ken a second glance as they moved toward the stage.

And right there, on the center of the stage, speaking into a mic, was Jordan Katz.

He was tall and balding, with sallow skin, but he held himself like he was confident and handsome even though he wasn't much of a looker. Damn. Going up there would cause a huge scene. She needed to get him off that stage.

"Now," Jordan said into the mic. Everyone near the stage was watching and listening. "I'd like everyone to give it up for my uncle, Officer Frank Katz!"

A tall, broad officer strolled onto the stage, waving.

"Holy shit," Nicky said, "he's related to someone on the force."

"Figures," Ken said. He pulled on Nicky's arm, pulling her toward the stage.

"I know you're going to enjoy this," Jordan said. "I went to his retirement party recently, and I saw the man eat three plates of food! Isn't that wonderful?"

Everyone laughed.

"So, as a token of my appreciation for all the years of service," Jordan said. "I've taken the liberty to plan him a wonderful retirement party. I'd like to officially welcome everyone to the party!"

Cheers went up.

"To hell with it," Ken said. Nicky looked at him, confused. "Let's just nail this son of a bitch to the ground."

"Walker, wait--"

But Ken was already storming up to the stage. Nicky had a bad feeling about this. She chased after.

As the two agents walked on stage, confusion took over the room. Ken and Nicky held their badges up.

"FBI!" Ken's voice boomed. "Jordan Katz, we need to speak to you!"

"What?" Jordan exclaimed, his face pale.

But it was Frank who stepped up to Ken. "What the hell are you feds doing here ruining my retirement party?"

"Step aside," Ken said. "We're taking Jordan Katz with us."

"Like hell you are. You're not taking anyone," Frank said, stepping even closer to Ken.

"If you don't get the hell out of my way," Ken said, "I will arrest you."

Frank's face flushed red. "You try that, you little prick, and I swear to God I will make sure you spend the rest of your life in prison."

Nothing happened for a moment, but then Ken stepped even closer to Frank, their faces inches apart.

"I'm not kidding," Ken said.

Frank's giant fist flung at Ken's face, hitting him right in the eye.

The whole room gasped. Chaos unleashed. But all Nicky could think of was Jordan--who was using the chaos to slip off stage, into the crowd.

Not on my watch, Nicky thought. Ken was a big guy--he could handle himself, so Nicky dashed past him and Frank as they duked it out and tailed Jordan through the crowd.

He was moving fast, but Nicky was faster. She'd been trained for this, and she was in top shape.

She knew how to run, and she knew how to run fast. She'd always been an athlete, and she'd always excelled at sports, and she knew she had the potential to be one of the best agents.

"Jordan Katz, FBI!" she yelled.

Despite what was going on, people cleared out of her way. Most of them had no idea what was happening, but they must've known that she was serious.

Nicky saw Jordan reach the back of the room, heading for the exit. She changed paths, bolting toward the door. She got there a few seconds before him, and she yanked it open.

He stood there, his eyes wide. "No!" he shouted, but it was too late. Nicky was ready. She leapt toward him, and he fell forward, tripping over his feet.

She jumped on top of him. He tried to fight back, but Nicky knew exactly how to pin someone down. She pulled her cuffs out and slammed them on his wrists.

The door opened behind her. Moments later, Ken appeared with what was definitely going to become a black eye. Nicky hauled Jordan to his feet.

"You're going to regret this," Jordan said, still trying to spit out threats to her, but she didn't even acknowledge him.

Ken grabbed Jordan's elbow and held him still. "We're going to get you for this," Jordan said, his face growing red.

"Give it up, Katz," Nicky said.

"You don't know what you're messing with," Jordan said.

"I've never been more sure of anything in my life," Ken said. He helped Nicky haul Jordan toward the car.

"We'll see about this," Jordan said. "I'm going to sue the FBI. You're going to be sorry you messed with me."

"You'll be in jail before you have a chance," Nicky said.

The other police officers were looking at the scene, maybe considering going in to stop them, but they never did. Good move. Nicky shoved Jordan Katz into the back of the rental car.

In that moment, she realized that she'd done it. She'd followed the case through, hunted down the criminal, and arrested him. She'd actually done it.

Now, all she had to do was get Katz to confess.

CHAPTER NINETEEN

Nicky stormed into the interrogation room at the Frankstown police station; it was nothing short of a dank, unimpressive box, but Nicky didn't care. She was ready to get Katz to fess up.

Ken was right beside her, and they both sat down across from Jordan Katz, who was fidgeting on the other side of the interrogation table. His hands were still cuffed behind his back, and he was still wearing his suit from the black-tie event. If Nicky had her way, the next thing he'd be wearing would be a prison jumper.

"Mr. Katz," Nicky said. "Are you ready to talk to us now?"

"I don't know what the hell this is about!" Katz yelled. "Why am I here?"

"You know why," Nicky said.

"No, really, I don't."

Exchanging a look with Nicky, Ken pulled out a file, took out a photo of Meghan Salinger, and slid it across the table.

"Do you recognize this woman, Jordan?" Nicky asked.

Jordan looked away. "Never seen her in my life."

"Are you sure about that? Because you matched with her on a dating app."

"What? No I didn't. Even if I did, so what? I get thousands of matches."

Nicky's eyes narrowed. She was getting closer.

"Mr. Katz," Nicky said, "this is Meghan Salinger. She went missing six months ago. Are you sure you don't remember her?"

"I don't have any idea what you're talking about," Jordan said. "I have to go. You can't keep me here."

"Mr. Katz," Nicky said, "you're not going anywhere. You've been arrested for the kidnapping of Meghan Salinger."

"That's bullshit! You can't arrest me for that. I'm innocent! You don't have any evidence."

"You're not innocent," Ken said, "but you are going to tell us everything you know about Meghan Salinger's disappearance."

"You're not giving me a choice here, are you? Well, I hate to break it to you, but I don't know squat about this chick or what happened to her."

Ken leaned forward, staring into Jordan's eyes. "Is that so? Maybe it's time we revealed to you exactly what it is that's going to happen to you if you don't talk to us."

"I'm not even listening to you!" Jordan said. He raised his voice, looking around the room. "You can't keep me here!"

Nicky's patience was running thin. She took out the file with a photo of one of the other victims and flung it at Katz.

"This is Ella White. Do you remember her?"

"No!"

"What about Teresa Simmons? Do you remember her?"

Once again, Katz screamed, "No!"

"Well, Mr. Katz," Nicky said. "It's time to remember."

Ken slammed the file down on the table. It landed with a thud. "It's time you remembered."

"I'm not listening to you."

"Tell us what we need to know," Nicky said. "I guarantee that you're going to wish you were dead before it's all over if you don't."

"I'm not going to talk to you," Katz said, "because I don't know shit about any of these women!"

"You do," Nicky said. "You matched with Meghan. You met her. But when you saw each other in real life, you didn't look like your photos, did you? And you're much older than you claim to be online."

Katz was sweating now, brown eyes flicking between Ken and Nicky. "That's not true."

"You're not getting out of this one," Nicky said. "We know everything we need to know about you, Mr. Katz. And I will tell you this: we know for a fact that you were going to kill Meghan Salinger, like you killed all these other women. Where's Meghan, Jordan?"

"I don't know what you're talking about!"

Nicky stopped herself from pushing on. Of course, turning on the aggression and acting like she already knew he was guilty was a tactic that worked in some cases, but not others. Here, she was desperate, and that was coming through in her work.

But there were also a couple things that didn't add up. For one, if he had Meghan, and abducted his new victim earlier today, why was he at a black-tie event?

Meghan went missing months ago, so confirming his alibi for then would be hard. But they could still figure out where he was earlier today.

"Where were you earlier, Jordan?" Nicky asked.

"I was working an open house," he said.

"And did anyone come by?"

"Well, no, but--"

"No one came by?" Nicky asked. "Can anyone confirm if you were actually there?"

Jordan's face turned red. He looked away. "It wasn't exactly a hot property. No one showed up. But I promise you, I was there all day. Maybe someone did see me, I don't know."

"That's not good enough, Jordan," Ken said. "Maybe no one can tell us where you were because you were abducting your next victim."

"What? No. I mean, of course. I wouldn't do that."

"And why was that?" Nicky asked. "Because you can't get the women you'd already abducted out of your system? And it occurred to you that you could target someone new?"

"That's not true!"

"You're a killer," Ken said. "You've done this before. And you're going to kill Meghan Salinger. I have no doubt."

"No one's going to believe that."

"They will, Jordan," Ken said.

"This is all crazy talk," Jordan said. "When I get out of here, I'm gonna sue you two so hard. You really messed with the wrong guy."

A knock at the door cut the interrogation short. Nicky looked over her shoulder to see Sheriff Corbin, looking grim. "You two. We need to talk. Now."

Nicky shot Jordan a look before she and Ken met with the sheriff in the hall. The sheriff eyed them up. If the FBI wasn't all over this, Nicky was sure he wouldn't be so keen on relaying information, but he was being cooperative enough now.

"We just got word that Katz's properties have been searched extensively," Corbin said. "There's no sign of either of the missing women."

Nicky's stomach dropped. That didn't sound good. "They've been checking everywhere?" Nicky asked.

"Yeah. My team, plus some of yours from the FBI, have got a whole team searching for Meghan Salinger and the other girl. They've got a dog unit and everything. I know Katz personally--his uncle Frank Katz is a good man. But let's put that aside for a second, because as you both know, this is out my hands now that you feds are involved."

Nicky could tell this was the biggest ego blow of Corbin's career, but she couldn't care less about that.

Corbin went on, "Katz only owns one property. Your friends at the FBI are looking into every property he's currently representing too. No sign of the girls anywhere."

"Then he has them somewhere else," Ken said. "I don't care if you think his uncle's a good guy. His uncle is the one who gave me this black eye," Ken said, gesturing to the swelling on his left eye. "Either way, Katz is connected to Meghan, and he has a long history of assault. He's our guy, Sheriff. I'm sorry."

But even as Ken was saying that, Nicky wasn't all that convinced.

Some things definitely did not add up with Katz. She'd been so convinced it was him before, but now she wasn't so sure. The more she thought about it, the more she was starting to realize it didn't make sense.

She needed to talk to Ken alone, so she said to the sheriff, "Thanks, Corbin. We'll let you know if we need anything else. Katz stays here for now."

Begrudgingly, Corbin nodded and took off, leaving Nicky and Ken alone in the hall.

"Well, what should we do?" Ken asked. "We have probably cause to arrest him, that's for sure, and I know we'll find evidence soon."

Nicky chewed on her lip. "Walker, I'm not so sure he's our guy."

"What?" He lifted an eyebrow.

"I don't know. Maybe he's not the one. We don't have any physical evidence yet."

Ken crossed his arms and scowled. "But he has a direct connection to Meghan and the warehouse. Everything points to him."

"I know that." Even as Nicky was saying it, she doubted herself. "Its just not right, Ken. If he'd just freshly kidnapped a new victim, then why bother with the black-tie event? Why wouldn't he do it on a day where he's not busy? And if he were trying to cover it up and give himself an alibi, why wouldn't he be smart enough to secure one for earlier? Get one of his police buddies to lie for him?"

"I don't know. Maybe he's hotheaded. Maybe he's desperate. Maybe he's planning on killing her and taking off right after."

"I don't know," Nicky said. "Something about this doesn't feel right."

"We've got plenty of time to check him out," Ken said. "I'm not letting him go."

"I know." Nicky stared at the floor. "But what if we're wrong? If we are, then..."

"It's a big risk. I know."

Nicky nodded. But this was her team—she was in charge, and she got to call the shots. She just hoped Ken would have her back. She said, "Let's keep him in custody, but keep searching other leads, okay?"

"All right," Ken said. "I can agree on that."

Nicky was glad they could come to a consensus. But she couldn't shake the feeling of anxiety in her gut.

If the killer was still out there, then he'd realize soon that he'd lost his kill basement. The police and FBI were all over it looking for DNA and clues, but Nicky knew she'd get a call the moment something came up. They were also staking the place out, just in case he hadn't already seen the commotion. There were officers and agents patrolling the area at all hours.

But still.

The guy could slip by. And if he did still intend on killing Meghan, and he picked up his new victim today, then that likely meant Meghan was due to die tonight.

If the killer didn't have his basement, where would he go?

He'd likely want another spot similar to the warehouse, as it had been working for him for so long.

Bernard Brown's message slid back into Nicky's mind.

So far, the word "home" had led her down several paths. Maybe it could lead her down another.

"What are you thinking, Lyons?" Ken asked.

She frowned. "I'm thinking we need to look for other abandoned buildings with the word 'home' in their title. Defunct businesses like Home Furniture."

It could be a shot in the dark, but Nicky was used to taking those. Sometimes it worked, sometimes it didn't.

But this one needed to work. Meghan's life depended on it.

"I think we should call Grace on this one," Nicky said.

CHAPTER TWENTY

The stars were slowly emerging, one by one, from behind the dark clouds. Nicky tore out of the police station's parking lot, Ken in the passenger seat. The tires screeched and the engine roared, the car leaving dust in its wake. Grace, the tech genius she was, had pulled up two potential matches within thirty seconds. One old abandoned apartment building called 'Sunrise Homes,' that had shut down after a bad fire, and another old warehouse of a defunct business that was once called 'Home Furniture Factory.' The latter was the most similar to the other location, so Nicky had her sights set on that one first.

Maybe it was a longshot, but she had to try. There was no losing here. Katz was in custody, so if he was the killer, he wouldn't be able to finish the job anytime soon. If he wasn't the killer, though, then it was worth looking further into.

The only thing Nicky wished was that this car could drive faster. She was already running the damn thing into the ground.

Nicky was driving fast down the highway, the night's darkness quickly overtaking her.

"Lyons," Ken said.

Nicky glanced at him.

"We're gonna find her," he said. "One way or another."

Emotion struck her chest. "There's only one good way to find her and that's alive."

"I know," he said, "and I agree. But if we don't..."

"There's no if we don't. We find her alive. That's it."

Ken didn't reply, but Nicky knew how she was behaving. She knew that nothing could ever guarantee a missing person being found alive. She knew that most missing persons were never found at all.

But she couldn't deal with another Masie. And so, she blocked out the idea that it was even possible. Meghan was alive, and Nicky would find her.

As she drove, she tried to calm the steady thud of her heart, but she found herself going back to the place she always went back to. The place where her worst memories existed, but also the place that somehow brought her the most comfort. In this place, Rosie was alive, and they were together—no matter the circumstances.

The lake house. Rosie. The man.

It all took over, until Nicky couldn't stop herself from becoming immersed in the memory, even with the lights of the highway ahead of her windshield.

***

"We need to get out of here," Rosie said.

Nicky shivered, sitting on the floor of the cold, empty cabin.

"He could be out there still," Nicky had said.

She was the older one. She was the one who should have been in charge. But she was scared. Scared that the wrong move could cause them to lose their lives.

They'd been in the cabin for three days now with nothing to eat but a few stale crackers, and a bucket for a toilet. He came and went, only to check in on them, ask how they were doing, and smile. He always smiled.

They'd tried the door many times, but it was too well-locked. There was no other exit.

They were trapped. He'd boarded up every window, every nook and cranny that they could possibly try to break free from. Plus, without being able to see outside, they couldn't tell when he was there and when he wasn't. Sometimes they'd hear his tires crunch over the gravel, signaling that he'd left, but he'd always come back soon. Always.

This was one of those nights. They'd heard his tires leave a half an hour ago, and as always, had tried to figure a way out. But they couldn't. He'd never been gone for more than thirty minutes before.

Nicky's mind raced as she looked around the dark and empty cabin. They'd tried removing nails from one of the windows so they could get to the other side, but it was hard for their small fingers to do without tools. But three days of slowly picking at them was starting to work, and if they were going to do it, maybe now was the best time.

"We need to try again," Rosie said.

Tears welled in Nicky's eyes. She was so scared, so scared they would die, so scared they were going to be trapped in this prison forever, so scared they wouldn't be able to find the strength to open the door and leave, so scared that maybe she'd be too scared to do it, and the door would stay shut, and they would be stuck here in this cabin for the rest of their lives, never being able to find the courage to open the door, never being able to find the strength to leave.

106

She took a deep breath. She had to be brave. She couldn't let him win. She couldn't let him take away her self-worth, her dignity, her pride, her will to live.

"Okay," she said, hoping her voice sounded stronger than she felt. "Okay, let's do it."

Nicky managed to break a window with a piece of wood, and she and Rosie had been able to crawl out, moving slowly and quietly so they wouldn't attract attention, just in case the man was somehow still around.

They were moving through the woods together now, moving as fast as they could. Each step was a risk, but they had to get out of this forest, get away from this man.

"I can't feel my feet," Rosie said.

"We need to keep going," Nicky said. "We're almost there, we can—Rosie?"

Rosie didn't answer.

She was gone.

The moon was out, but it wasn't bright enough to see far ahead. Nicky turned around and around, but she couldn't find Rosie.

"Rosie!" she whispered. "Rosie!"

There was no reply. Nicky looked back at the cabin, which was still visible through the trees. It was farther away than she had thought. She had never been so far away from it, not since the first day they came here.

Then, suddenly, there was light.

Headlights.

He was back.

"Rosie!" Nicky shouted.

"I'm stuck!" she heard her yell.

"Where? I can't see you!" Everywhere was dark. But the sound of the man's wheels crunching over the path to the cabin was getting closer by the second.

Nicky ran as fast as she could, dodging tree roots and trying to stay quiet.

The car pulled up to the cabin, and the man got out. He was holding a gun. Nicky was out of time. She had no choice but to stay hidden.

"Rosie, where are you?" Nicky whispered.

No response.

Nicky peered between the foliage to see the man had noticed they'd broken out.

He was staring at the empty window.

There was a flash of light--a flashlight.

The man was looking for them.

"Rosie, please, I can't find you!" Nicky whispered.

Another flash of light.

Then, Nicky heard Rosie scream.

She could see her now--the man was dragging her out of the forest, toward the cabin. She kicked and screamed, but he was too strong.

Nicky froze in place, terrified.

She could still get away. But that would mean leaving Rosie.

I'll get help, she told herself. I have to get help.

She ran as fast as her legs would carry her, away from her sister-- away from the cabin.

She had no idea what was going to happen to them. She didn't know what he was going to do. But she knew she needed to get away.

The forest was menacing in the dead of night. Nicky tore through the trees. The canopy of trees blocked most of the moonlight. The blackness of the forest was a blanket, smothering her. Leaves and pine needles crackled under her feet, like a thousand men stomping through the woods.

Nicky's fear was breaking through the adrenaline. It tasted bitter. She could feel it choking her.

This was real. Whatever had happened during those three days changed her life forever. She didn't want to go back there. She didn't want to be that girl anymore. She didn't want to have to cope with those memories. She didn't want to know what had happened between her and that man.

Nicky struggled to breathe. It wasn't just a physical struggle--it was something inside her. She could feel it, deep within her. She could feel her body resisting her.

But finally, she made it to the road.

She was in the middle of the woods, and the only thing she could see was the vast, open wilderness in all directions. The only thing she could hear was the soft rustle of leaves and the occasional birdcall. The only thing she could feel was the cool, refreshing breeze on her skin and the sturdy earth beneath her feet. She was alone and unprotected and there was nothing she could do to get help if she needed it.

She started walking, staggering a little, trying not to trip on the uneven road. She knew where she was going. She had to find someone, anyone. She had to find help.

So she walked, and walked, and walked, and the whole time, not a single car passed.

It wasn't until a light appeared ahead that Nicky began to feel hope.
It was a gas station.

There was a convenience store attached, and a few cars parked out front.

The light was bright, and as she got closer, she saw that it was a sign, written in large, red letters:

OPEN 24 HOURS

Nicky could see the outline of a man standing behind the counter, and she saw the glow of a cigarette. She walked inside, the bell above the door jingling to alert him she was there.

She eased over to the counter, but the man didn't look up. He was sitting on a stool, reading a newspaper, a cigarette dangling from his lips.

Nicky cleared her throat, but still, the man didn't look up. He didn't seem to notice her standing there. Nicky was about to ask if she could use the phone when he turned his head. He stared at her curiously, letting the cigarette fall to the floor and extinguishing it with his shoe.

"Please," she begged. "The police. I need the police."

That was when the man stood up, realizing this was serious.

The next few hours were a blur. Police arrived. Nicky's parents were called. And Nicky had to lead them back to the cabin by memory.

All the way there, she wasn't sure if it was real. It seemed like a dream. She was walking and seeing things she knew weren't there. She saw the man in the woods, calling her name. She saw Rosie in a ditch. She saw the cabin, abandoned, dark and quiet, and she heard angry, guttural moans from inside.

But when they arrived, the cabin was just as they had left it. The man's van was gone. That was the first red flag.

Nicky pointed out the cabin where the man had taken Rosie, the muddy tracks leading up the deck, and she told them everything she could.

But it was only minutes before the police turned back around.

"Sorry," one officer said. "There's no sign of any girl here."

Rosie was never seen again.

***

Nicky came back from the memory as the exit on the highway came up. The moon and stars shone above, their luminescence blurred by the interstate lights. The sky was a deep blue, and the stars looked like diamonds on the black velvet backdrop.

It wasn't the first time she'd gone into full memory mode while running on auto pilot. It wouldn't be the last. She turned the wheel and took a right off the highway, onto a dark road. In the passenger seat, she could feel Ken's eyes on her.

"You haven't talked in at least twenty minutes," Ken said. "That's not like you, Lyons."

"Sorry," she said. "I was just thinking."

"About what?"

Nicky didn't reply. She'd already revealed too much to Ken the other night in the hotel. He was going to start thinking she was too soft, even though she wasn't. Nicky's memories, her PTSD--she didn't consider them a weakness. She considered them a strength.

"What's going on?" Ken asked.

"I'm not soft or anything," Nicky clarified. She wasn't being rude, just wanted to gently let him know that he didn't need to worry. And maybe she did care about earning his respect.

"I never said you were," Ken replied.

"I know." Nicky kept driving for a moment. "Was just thinking about what happened again. That's all."

"With your sister."

Nicky nodded with a lump in her throat.

"It's not your fault," Ken said. "You didn't know what was going to happen. And you were a kid too."

"Yeah, but I was her big sister." She paused, her voice thick. "I shouldn't have been the one to get away."

"I get that." Ken looked out the window. "You're the only one in the office I've told about what happened to Tiana."

Nicky paused. She didn't know that. But Ken was far from an open book, so that made sense. Working with Ken had changed her opinion of him. He'd always seemed to aggressive and rude in the office, and in many ways, petty and jealous. But that wasn't Ken Walker at all. Like her, he was in this to save lives, maybe to repent for the people they both couldn't save.

"I won't tell anyone about your story," Nicky said. "It's between us."

He nodded. "Thanks, Lyons."

Ken fell silent, and the rest of the ride was quiet as well. But Nicky was too wound up. She fiddled with the radio, trying to find a station that wasn't playing any bad music. She finally settled on a classic rock station, which was playing "Bad Moon Rising" by Creedence.

She seemed to always choose songs that brought up memories.

110

She glanced over at Ken, who was still listening to the radio. He looked grim and detached, with his eyes on the road. She wondered if he ever went off into his own world, like hers. Into a world where his friend was still alive. A world that hurt in the most addictive way.

Quietly, Nicky continued driving down the long, dark road, and hoped this one would lead to absolution for herself, Ken--and Meghan.

CHAPTER TWENTY ONE

His hands trembled against the wheel of the car.

Everything was going horribly wrong.

He couldn't believe it. Not only had his last fiancé failed her vows, but now he had nowhere to get rid of her. Until he disposed of his last pathetic excuse for a bride, then he couldn't give his true love the ceremony she deserved. He was nothing, if not faithful.

He was back on the highway now, and his ex-bride was still in the trunk, still kicking, still screaming. In backseat behind him, gagged and bound, was his new woman, his new love.

He had the jitters as he met her bulging eyes in the rear-view mirror. "Don't worry, dear! I told you I'd get rid of her. I promise!"

She made some noise through her gag. He was disappointing her. No, no, he couldn't do that.

"I'm sorry, sweetheart! I promise she'll be gone, and we can be together!"

His true love only cried more. He hated seeing her in pain.

He punched the steering wheel. Damn it! He needed to get rid of his ex-bride, who was causing his new bride so much pain. He turned on the radio for the fourth time in as many minutes, but there was no news to report. He tried to relax, but the slightest movement only caused the screaming in the trunk to increase.

He turned the radio off.

Relax, he told himself. So, his old spot was no good. But it wasn't like he didn't have a backup plan. What was he, a fool? Of course not. He would get rid of his filthy ex-bride and he would do it quickly.

A smile curled at his lips.

This was going to be easy.

Turning up the music, he sang along to his favorite song, and tried to clear his mind of everything except the music. He was going to be a good husband to his wife, they would be a good couple, not like his parents. Not like Mother.

The song was the one he had sung at his last wedding, and though it had seemed forever, it was only four minutes. The song ended and the announcer came on. "That one, that one is for the beautiful bride and groom."

"Oh, shut up!" he muttered bashfully. "You're too kind. We're technically not married yet!"

He changed the station to classical music, because it reminded him of Mother.

He remembered the way Mother would keep him in the basement for hours, all the windows shut, never letting him leave. And she would whisper to him through the door, telling him how much she loved him. How much he meant to her. How much she would never hurt him. How much he was the only one she could ever truly love.

She was so lonely after Father was no longer around. But Mother made it clear that he, he could never leave her. He was hers.

But he had escaped Mother, and now he was free to live his own life, to choose his own love. He was no longer the little boy who had listened to the classical music she played in the basement of their home. He was a man. He had a new love, a new wife. He did not need to listen to the soft songs that reminded him of his mother's voice.

He changed to an old country song he used to sing with his father on the old acoustic guitar.

The song was about love, but it was about love lost. A man sang the song to the woman who had destroyed his love, and though she stood in front of him, she was no longer the beautiful bride he had married. He had no more use for her, because he had found love again with his new wife-to-be. Only this time, she was completely different.

He wiped his eyes. He was being foolish. A good man should forget such things and focus on what was important.

And right now, the only important thing was getting rid of his ex-bride.

And he knew just the place.

A home away from home...

CHAPTER TWENTY TWO

Nicky's heart fell to the floor.

The old warehouse was demolished. All of it. The remains of the building were spread out in front of her, under the night sky. The bricks and mortar lay in shattered pieces on the ground. The wooden beams and support posts had been torn down, leaving nothing but splinters and rubble in their wake. The once-solid structure now looked like a skeleton, stretched out on the ground in front of her.

Beside her, Ken let out a whistle. "Something tells me this isn't where he's going."

Nicky's hands shook. "Grace said it was here, but the internet probably hadn't updated yet. This demolition was recent." Nicky could tell by the way the track marks from the machinery were still embedded in the earth.

Nicky paused. Took a moment to breathe, collect herself. The air was cool, as if it had just rained. The crickets sang all around them, their high-pitched notes weaving in and out of each other, as if they were trying to create a melody. The road stretched out before them, a narrow, pitted path that disappeared into the darkness. They were way off the highway, and the only light came from the stars and the moon.

Okay, so this was the wrong spot. And they were running out of time. But Nicky couldn't let this defeat her.

The only way forward was up.

"We don't have time to waste." Nicky hurried back over to the car and hopped behind the wheel. Ken followed, buckling into the passenger side.

With that, Nicky floored it. Destination: the next location, Sunrise Homes, the old apartment building.

They screeched over the bridge and onto the interstate again, heading toward the first leg of their trip.

The GPS on the car's dash said they were twenty minutes away. Nicky white-knuckled the wheel. It couldn't be too late. Not after she'd gotten so close. She needed to save Meghan, and she needed to hurry. Every second she wasted was another foot in Meghan Salinger's grave.

Keep it together, Lyons, she told herself.

It's almost over.

114

She took the exit ramp for the interstate and turned onto the street.

Shadows stretched across the road ahead, but she couldn't see much, as the headlights didn't quite reach the end of the road. She bounced off a few potholes, and it felt like she was fleeing for her life.

Almost there. Almost there.

Minutes passed that felt like an eternity. She pulled up to the desolate parking lot of what used to be an apartment building on the outskirts of Frankstown. It was dark, but Grace had told her about the place, and she knew where it was. She only hoped it actually was the right spot.

The dilapidated building was old and worn, with peeling paint and faded lettering on the sign. Char from the fire was visible on the bottom half. The vines were growing up the side, twining around the window frames and curling around the door handles. The building looked abandoned, as if it had been forgotten by the world. The sign that read 'Sunrise Homes' was faded and cracked.

"This place is deserted," Ken muttered.

Nicky nodded. "It's the last place on earth I want to be."

After parking, she stepped out of the car and gazed at the building. The windows were either gone or smashed in, and there was not a soul was in sight. As Nicky and Ken walked across the lot, their footsteps echoed.

But as Nicky made it closer to the building, something off to the side of it gleamed in the moonlight.

The trunk of a car emerged. It was a black sedan.

"Shit," Nicky said. Her heart leapt into her throat. "Ken. Someone's here."

"Jesus," Ken said. "It could be him. Be careful."

Nicky couldn't believe it. All this time, she'd been chasing Meghan Salinger. And now, if she were right, then Meghan was here. This was why she'd become an FBI agent.

I can still save you.

Ken had his gun out as they went up to the car, slowly, checking their surroundings, but there was nothing but the old lot and the trees surrounding it.

But as they got closer to the car, they heard a sound.

A thumping sound.

Nicky's pulse roared.

"Someone's in the trunk."

The thumping got louder. Nicky exchanged a look with Ken before they both hurried up to the vehicle.

Someone screamed something unintelligible from inside.

Meghan. Nicky's chest wouldn't stop thudding. This was it. She'd found Meghan. She'd found her alive.

"Ken, we need to get this thing open," Nicky said.

"I'm on it." Ken went to the driver door, and with his gun, he punched the window. It shattered, echoing through the night. Nicky hovered her sweaty hands over the trunk of the car, waiting for Ken to pop the trunk.

He did it.

And they were in.

A woman was inside of the trunk, bound and gagged. Redhead. This had to be Meghan. Her eyes watered at the sight of them, and when Nicky reached out to her, the woman broke into sobs. Nicky removed the gag.

Only to see that this wasn't Meghan at all. This was the new girl, Lauren Klein.

"Oh, God, help me!" Lauren cried.

"It's okay. It's okay." Nicky whispered to her. "We're here to help you."

Nicky didn't mean to seem disappointed—she was glad Lauren was okay, but if Meghan wasn't in the car, then Nicky feared that what she'd been most afraid of was coming true.

She feared that Meghan was already dead

Lauren's eyes widened. "That crazy bastard, he--"

"Was there another woman with him?" Nicky asked desperately. "Was she with you?"

"Yes!" Lauren screamed. "He's going to kill her! He went inside the building!"

Jesus Christ, Nicky thought. She had to move.

"Lyons, go," Ken said, taking out his phone. "I'll stay with her and call backup. Get in there. Save her."

Nicky didn't think any more. She just ran. Ran toward the apartment building, terrified of what she'd find inside. She burst through an open door, finding herself in the lobby of what used to contain people's homes. Now, the walls were all broken in, exposing the various units. And the smell was putrid, like mildew and dead animals. Plus, the stench of the fire that had happened so many years ago somehow still lingered.

She could make out the shape of an open door on the left, which led to what used to be the living room. The room was dark, but as Nicky made her way toward the door, she thought she could hear movement. She walked faster, her heart in her throat.

The door was ajar. It was a hall, and it led to an apartment kitchen. She followed it, but as soon as she was in the kitchen, she stopped to listen.

Nothing.

And no one was out there. It was just the draft penetrating the broken-down walls.

She opened the door and stepped into the hall. The door swung shut behind her. As she did, she saw the room. The kitchen was a sad mess of dirty, broken dishes, and filthy pots and pans littered the floor.

Where was he? He was here, somewhere, but where? Meghan was here too. Nicky had to save her. She wouldn't let her die, she wouldn't let her become another victim of this man, who had already stolen so many lives.

Nicky hurried back into the main hallway, where dust had settled on the floor.

But that wasn't all.

There were footprints.

Someone had been there.

Then Ken's voice came over her earpiece. "Nicky, where are you? What's going on?"

She followed the footsteps down the hallway, toward a metal door at the end of the hall.

"Nicky, we're coming in," he said. "Just hang on."

The sign on the door read: BOILER ROOM.

But Nicky couldn't wait. She opened the door. A set of stairs appeared before her, leading into the inky black.

For a moment, Nicky hesitated.

She knew she might not like what she'd find down there. But she had to do this.

She wasn't able to save Masie, but this was her chance to right that wrong.

A breath, and she went down.

There were no lights. It was pitch black. Nicky's eyes adjusted to the darkness, but it made the place feel even more disorienting. The air was filled with a cloying smell of something rancid. She couldn't help but think that whoever had been here before the fire had left in a hurry.

Her footsteps echoed down the stairs, and she could just make out the faint sounds of something moving around farther down, like something was in the boiler room.

Nicky's throat tightened.

Rosie's face flared up in her mind.

She remembered the way she looked before the man had caught her again.

Before Nicky had run off.

All this time, Rosie had been off somewhere--who knows where? Maybe she was dead, maybe he still had her alive. Either way, Nicky had been able to get away. Live a full life. Become an agent. Have a life. Maybe she didn't do enough with it.

Rosie had always wanted a boyfriend, Nicky remembered. But Nicky had never had one, not for real. In fact, if a man ever tried to get too close to her, she was more likely to kick them to the curb. Then she'd find herself lonely late at night, but still unable to open herself up to any real intimacy.

She knew that if Rosie had the chances that Nicky had, she wouldn't take them for granted.

Every day, Nicky felt more regret, more pain and anguish for leaving her sister behind and escaping. Who would Rosie have become? If Rosie had been saved too, would Nicky still be an agent? She felt like she was meant to be, in her blood, but she'd give everything up if it meant her sister could be free, having a safe life.

Nicky refocused herself as she walked, gun up and ready, on full alert.

This wasn't the same as all those years ago. Nicky wasn't a child anymore. She was an agent.

This time, Nicky would win.

As she made her way through the boiler room, the air started hitting her more and more. It smelled less like mildew now, more like something else.

She came upon a large, red door with a sign above it: COALING AREA. She moved toward it, just as the thumping sound in the room became louder, whatever it was now coming toward her.

She raised her gun, ready to shoot. But just as she did, she dimly made out the shape of a person. The movement was familiar.

As she got closer, a sliver of moonlight slipped in through a hole in the burned ceiling. It took her mind a moment to process what she was seeing.

A man was holding a red-haired woman by her neck, and she was wearing a wedding dress.

But she was alive. Standing. Struggling against him.

Nicky couldn't bask in the relief, not yet.

"My poor, stupid bride," the man cried. "You were the one for me... the one..."

What the hell? Nicky didn't know what she was seeing, but it was beyond bizarre. She'd never seen anything like this, not in her entire time of being a federal agent.

Nicky stepped forward, and her foot hit a rock.

The man's head snapped to her.

CHAPTER TWENTY THREE

His crazed eyes gleamed against the moonlight, pointed right at Nicky. She held her gun firm, directed right at his face.

"Don't you fucking move," she said.

He was vile. His hair was greasy and bone-white. His eyebrows bushy and black. His skin was gray, his clothes stinking. And he was covered in coal dust, which made him look even more disgusting.

The woman in the wedding dress looked at Nicky. Her eyes were still wide with fear.

But when Nicky locked eyes with her, she recognized her immediately.

This really was Meghan. And Nicky wasn't too late.

But something was wrong.

Meghan looked like she was in an awful lot of pain. Her face was covered in bruises, and her eyes sunken. She looked like hell. Nicky gritted her teeth. But before Nicky could make a clear shot at him, he spun Meghan in front of him, still holding her throat with his hand.

"You wouldn't shoot my bride," the man said. "If you do that, you'll kill her."

Meghan made a gurgling noise as he clamped harder on her throat.

"That's enough," Nicky screamed. "I'll shoot you!"

But he was using Meghan as a human shield. That damn coward.

"If you kill me," he said, "you'll kill her too. That isn't what you want, is it?"

Nicky kept her gun aimed at him, but she couldn't pull the trigger. She was frozen, too afraid of what would happen if she shot--and missed. It was too risky. She had to buy time for Ken to get in here with backup. She had to keep this guy talking.

"Why are you doing this?" she asked.

"Because..." He sniggered, making Nicky's skin crawl. "Because I needed a bride. You know, you aren't so bad yourself... why don't you step into the light?"

Nicky's eyes squinted as she looked at him. "I'm not a bride," she said. "What are you talking about?" This man was a lunatic.

"I know you," he said, his eyes wandering over her body in a pervy way. "You look perfect..."

120

Sufficiently creeped out, Nicky prayed Ken would show up soon.

"Let her go or I'll put you down," Nicky said.

"You won't," he taunted. "If you do, I'll snap her neck."

Damn it. He had her pinned. Nicky had dealt with many intense situations in her life—but none had been as disturbing and nerve-wracking as anything she'd seen on this case. She just wanted it all to be over. She wanted everyone to walk away with their lives.

"Who are you?" she said, "and why do you want her?"

"I'll tell you," he said. "My name is Roy. You know, the way I see it, I'll get you to love me. And I'll get you to stay by my side. You'll have your family. And I'll have my bride. And we'll have a happy, simple life together."

So, this was his schtick. Based on the dress, he was obsessed with marriage. It looked like every time a bride "let him down," he put her down, replacing her with a new one. Nicky's stomach rolled. But something in his speech stood out of her. He didn't speak of vile acts-- he spoke of a happy life.

"Is that what you want, Roy?" she asked. "To be a good husband, to have a nice family?"

"Yes," he said. "And if you shoot me, I'll snap your bride's neck too."

Nicky looked at the wedding dress, back at Roy's face.

This guy was deranged. He must have been seriously messed up to search for a bride in the first place, to think he could find someone who would fit his stereotype of what a bride was supposed to look like.

"You wouldn't hurt your bride," Nicky said. She needed to get in his head. "No. You'll do anything to keep her alive, just like a real groom would."

"You're right," he said.

"She's a good woman," Nicky said. "She doesn't deserve this. You need help. You need someone who can help you."

"She's a cold little bitch," the man said. "She messed up our vows. Something as important as our vows, and she messed it all up!"

"If you let her go," Nicky said, "I can do something for you."

"I don't need help," he said. "I'm better off without her. She's always wanting more and more. She wants everything--"

"Doesn't that mean you're doing the same?" she said. "Taking advantage of women? Taking their bodies and using them as toys? They aren't dolls, Roy, they're people."

"Women are made to serve men," he said. "And I'm no fool. I can't take advantage of any woman. I'm too much of a gentleman for that. I want love."

"But why Meghan?" Nicky said. "You can let her go now, it's okay. Let her go, Roy."

"She'll be dead soon," he said. "I'll just let her burn. I make her suffer, but it's only because I love her."

He was sick. Talking wasn't going to cut it. Nicky needed to get Meghan away from him--even if that meant she had to kill this bastard.

She kept her gun aimed at him, ready to pull the trigger at any moment. He grinned at her, knowing he had the upper hand.

"Meghan didn't deserve this," Nicky said. "She's a good person. And I'm going to make sure she gets out of this alive."

"A real woman would try to get away with it," he said. "But not Meghan. She wouldn't try to run away. She'd just take it. She's the type of woman who'll take whatever I dish out. Because she wants to be a good wife."

He raised his hand and slapped Meghan across the face.

She gasped at the pain. Nicky's teeth grit. But she still didn't have a clear shot. *Damn it!*

"She'll never be a good wife!" he said. "She'll be a horrible one. She messed up our vows. I never should have trusted her!"

"Are you saying it was your fault?" Nicky asked.

"It wasn't," he said. "But I knew... I should have known. She doesn't care about the vows; she cares about the wedding night. She'll try to convince you that she'll keep her promise. But she'll soon realize what she's done. She'll realize she messed it all up. And then she'll try to run away. And then I'll snap her neck. You'll never see her again. I hate her, but that's only because I love her."

"That's not how love works," Nicky said. "Love makes you forgive."

"Love is everything," he said. "Love is what I'm owed. It's what was taken from me."

She knew he was insane. But she was getting glimpses into his psyche.

"If you're going to be with Meghan, you'll have to be good," she said. "You'll have to be a real husband. You'll have to love and trust her. Isn't that right?"

"She's unworthy of me."

This was going nowhere fast, and Nicky needed a plan. She wondered what had happened in his life to make him end up this way. Why was he so obsessed with love, but not just love--marriage?

Nicky wondered about his own parents. Maybe his father wasn't a good husband. Or maybe his mother had left him.

"What about your parents, Roy?" Nicky asked. "Did they get divorced? Did your mom leave your father? Did your dad love your mom?"

"No," he said. "My mom was great. My mom was the best wife."

"What about your dad? Did he love your mom?"

"No," he said. "I told you. My mom was a good wife. He couldn't keep up with her."

"What happened to them?" Every moment she kept him talking was bought time.

She needed to use that time to get Meghan away.

"They're in a better place," he said. "They're watching over me. They'll be with me as long as I need."

"But you're still hurting," she said. "You're not getting what you want. Losing her will do that. You're not getting the love; you're not getting the family. You're still hurting. Admit it."

"I don't care about my failures," he said. "I don't care about people like you."

"You don't see," she said. "You're hurting. Let me help you. Let the girl go."

"Never!" He gripped her tighter. Shit. Nicky was out of time.

Nicky took in the room, looking for something to spark her imagination, something she could use to get him to let her go.

She looked up. At the moonlight through the ceiling.

Then, it hit her.

Nicky raised her gun in the air. The man frowned. Meghan's eyes bulged as she whimpered.

Nicky fired two shots into the cracked ceiling right above Roy's head.

Crumbled concrete fell down. He was taller than Meghan, towering over her, so it hit him first. A light bit of rubble hit her, but Nicky had hit the perfect spot to only get Roy with the big chunk.

It worked. A chunk hit Roy's head, dazing him.

Nicky didn't waste a second. She dove in and shoved Meghan away, freeing her from Roy's grips. She screamed and ran off.

But it wasn't over for Nicky.

Roy was quick. He went straight for her. The next thing Nicky knew, she was seeing stars. Pain reverberated through her skull.

He'd hit her over the head with something. She was seeing double.

Her gun wasn't in her hand.

When she could see straight again, all she saw was Roy coming for her.

"You'll never get to Meghan," he said. "I'll do anything to protect her."

Nicky went to pull out her gun, but Roy hit her over the head a second time.

She fell over. Still seeing double, she couldn't tell if the pain was coming from the blow to the head or the fall.

She didn't know what was going on. But she knew one thing.

He was responsible for the sudden shift.

The man was getting closer. She had to fight him off, or he'd kill her.

"It's you," he said. With a crazed smile, he mounted her, wrapping his hands around his throat. No. Nicky tried to knee him, but it didn't work. "You're the one I've been looking for," he said. "You're my true love. It's been you all along."

His voice sounded like a nightmare. He was a maniac. He had a look in his eyes that Nicky had only ever seen on one person.

Her own captor.

"I'm not yours!" Nicky yelled.

"You are," he purred. "You will be. Forget the others. It's just you and me."

"That's not how it works," Nicky said. "How do you make a woman love you? How do you force a woman to stay with you? It's not real, Roy!"

"I can't win against you," he said. "There's something inside of you. Something strong. Something I can't take away."

He was talking pure nonsense. Nicky tried to push him off, but his weight was crushing down on her, clamping on her throat, and she couldn't catch a breath. Nicky started to see stars.

"You can't hate me," he said. "You can't hate me."

The maniac was whispering in her ear.

"You love me... you love me..."

Her vision faded to white.

Was this it?

Was it really ending for her, yet again?

124

She thought of dropping into that lake with her hands tied behind her back, the moonlight through the rippling surface of the lake...

At least back then, she was with Rosie.

She pretended she was back there now. With Rosie at her side. But she didn't think of the lake, not anymore. She imagined them at the beach, or in the pool, when they were kids. Reaching for each other's hands. Blowing bubbles...

I love you, Rosie, Nicky thought. *I'm so sorry I couldn't save you.*

The last thing she heard was the man's horrible voice, whispering, "And I love you too."

CHAPTER TWENTY FOUR

Air swept into Nicky's lungs. She gasped and grabbed at her neck. The boiler room basement materialized around her.

She was alive. Nicky's heart was pounding. She felt the rhythmic pulse racing in her chest. Her skin tingled.

But a struggle unfolded in front of her. It was Ken. He'd pulled Roy off her--but Roy dove at him like a rabid animal. Ken had his gun out, but Roy grabbed his arms and held them in place. A gunshot went off, sending ripples of pain through Nicky's eardrums.

Nicky tried to stand, but the pain in her head was excruciating. She was woozy. Her limbs felt heavy, as if they were numb. She got up and coughed. The air smelled of oil and sulfur. It was heavy and thick. She could smell the sweat and rotten gas emanating from the boiler.

A long deep inhale and exhale. The first breath in and the first breath out.

Then she pried herself up and looked around. The room was destroyed, covered in dust and broken glass. Her vision was distorted.

Help. You have to help.

Nicky watched, paralyzed. Roy punched Ken in the face. Ken fell backward.

And Roy was on Ken before Nicky knew what was happening. Roy's fist came down hard, hitting Ken in the nose. Blood flowed from the wound and pooled on the ground.

No.

She had to do something.

Nicky reached for her gun, but it wasn't there.

Ken was too thrown off by the punch to resist. Somehow, in the struggle, Roy had disarmed Ken--and now the gun was pointed right at him.

Roy aimed.

"For your love," he said.

He was going to fire.

But Nicky didn't think. She just dove into action. She tackled Roy, and the gun went off--but it hit the ceiling. The gunpowder burned her nose. The roof collapsed in on itself. She saw the ceiling crack, the beams bend and snap. Immediately, plaster fell sprinkled on top of them. The force of the shot was enough to knock them both off their feet.

Nicky slapped Roy's wrist in the perfect way to force him to drop the weapon--and she grabbed it. She stood up and pointed it right at him. Roy was on his knees, and he froze when he realized that she had the upper hand.

She aimed at his forehead.

His eyes were wild.

His smile, growing. Almost begging her to do it.

She could shoot him right here. He'd deserve it. He was an animal who needed to be put down after what he did.

She thought of the faces of all those dead women. Her eyes burned.

"You son of a bitch," she said.

"Do it, if you must, my love," he said.

Her hands shook. Behind her, Ken said, "Lyons, it's over."

"It's not over!" Nicky shouted. "People like him deserve to die!"

When she looked down at him, she didn't see Roy anymore.

She saw the man. The one who'd taken her and Rosie.

The amount of times Nicky had dreamed of killing that man. Of making him pay. Of taking away all his power. Of getting revenge for what he'd done to Rosie.

She could do it right here. Shoot this bastard. Put him down.

"I know," Ken said, "but we need to do this by the books."

Ken's sensible voice bled through. Nicky took a moment. She opened her eyes and looked down at Roy, really looked.

He was not her captor, or Rosie's. He was just some other sick bastard. Did he deserve to die? Yes. But Nicky was a federal agent. She did things by the books.

"He doesn't get the easy way out," Ken said. "He's gonna rot in jail for the rest of his miserable existence."

"That's right," Nicky said. She realized then that would be a worse punishment than death for him. "He'll never get married again."

Roy's eyes glossed over. "No! Just kill me! Kill me!"

"No." Nicky lowered the weapon. Ken came over and kicked Roy to the ground, slapping cuffs on his wrists. Nicky stood over him with her arms crossed.

It was over.

He was caught.

***

127

Nicky and Ken dragged Roy upstairs, into the parking lot, greeted by the night, just as the police were arriving. The night sky was ablaze with red and blue light. Police sirens wailed in the distance.

By Roy's car, Meghan and Lauren were alive, with blankets over their shoulders, being comforted and questioned by a female officer. Nicky let out a breath of relief. But still. None of it felt real. Was it really all over?

"You okay?" Ken asked.

"It's over," Nicky said. "Thank God. For once, everything's okay."

But there was more to do. A few FBI agents next to a black car spotted them, and Ken brought Roy over to them, shoving him into their custody. Roy stole one last look at Nicky before he was shoved in the back of the car.

Good riddance.

Nicky went over to Meghan and Lauren--and Meghan instantly threw herself at Nicky, hugging her tight.

"You saved my life!" she cried.

Nicky's heart swelled. She wasn't much of a hugger, but she hugged Meghan back, so grateful that this hadn't ended the way it did with Masie.

"I had to," Nicky said.

"I don't know how I can ever thank you," Meghan said, pulling away with tears in her eyes.

"You don't have to," Nicky said. "I'm just glad you're alive."

"We're both alive," Lauren said.

Meghan pulled back and looked at Nicky. "I can't believe you did it."

Nicky blinked back tears. In this moment, every heartbreak she'd been through as an FBI agent was worth it. She'd won. She'd saved the girl.

"Your parents will be so relieved to see you," Nicky said to Meghan. "I know they were worried sick."

"I miss them so much," Meghan said. "I can't believe they thought I was dead all this time. But I survived."

"So did I," Lauren said.

"Yeah," Nicky said. "We all did."

Meghan and Lauren smiled and hugged her again. Nicky sighed. She was so grateful.

"Agent Lyons," a booming male voice suddenly said. Nicky turned to see Sheriff Corbin, his hands looped to his belt. "Sorry to break up the moment. A word?"

Nicky looked at Meghan and Lauren. "You two are safe now. That man will never see the light of day again, I promise."

"Thank you," Meghan said. "Thank you."

Nicky nodded at them and strolled away with Sheriff Corbin. Compared to the first time she'd met him, the man was a lot less hostile. Nicky hoped that seeing a crime as real and horrific as this was enough to get his head on straight.

"Well, Sheriff," Nicky said, "I hope--"

"You don't have to lecture me, Agent Lyons. I know."

Nicky nodded. "Do things by the books from now on. The FBI might be keeping an eye on your precinct."

The sheriff laughed a belly laugh. "Well, we'll work on that, but there's one issue that you feds didn't exactly clean up. Frank Katz's nephew is innocent, and he's threatening to sue."

"Let him sue, then," Nicky said. "We'll deal with it. We had reasonable cause to arrest Jordan. And he ran from us when he saw us, which he shouldn't have done if he were innocent."

"Yeah, well, the kid's got issues, but he's not a killer." Corbin gazed off at the car that Roy was inside. Ken was talking to the other agents beside it. "To think all this time, something so horrific was happening... what you two found in that warehouse has to be one of the most gruesome things to ever happen in this part of the world."

"It was," Nicky agreed. "But it's over now."

"Anyway... I wanted to say thanks," Corbin said.

Nicky nodded. "It's my job, Sheriff."

The sheriff took off, and Nicky went to meet with Ken. He broke away from the other agents and met with her in front of the old apartment building. Nicky looked at it, taking in the burnt wood and brick, imagining what life was like here before the fire--maybe, long ago, this was a beautiful place to live.

Now it was all ashes and ruined dreams.

"Hey," Ken said. Nicky met his blue eyes and half-smiled. "You really saved my ass back there," Ken said.

"Are you kidding?" Nicky almost laughed. "That bastard was choking the life out of me until you came in."

"Yeah, but he would've shot me in the face if you hadn't acted. I almost died, but you had my back, Lyons. Thanks."

Nicky wasn't sure what to say. She was happy he was okay. That was all the thanks she needed. "You're welcome, Walker. Guess we don't make a half-bad team."

"Guess not."

They shared a lingering smile. Things felt good between them now. Maybe they weren't the best friends in the world, but Nicky had respect for him, and he had respect for her.

And Nicky would be happy to keep working with Ken at her side.

They'd won this case, but there were way more girls out there who had never been found.

CHAPTER TWENTY FIVE

"Well, you three really did it," Senator Amara Gregory said as she paced the front of the briefing room back in Jacksonville. Feeling proud, Nicky sat at the table with Ken, Grace, and Chief Franco.

"Told you they were fine agents," Chief Franco said.

"Agent Lyons and Agent Walker did all the hard work," Grace said, her cheeks flushed.

"No way," Nicky said. "Without your help, we would've taken way longer to figure out where we needed to be. Thanks, Grace."

"Well, I'm glad you all get along," Amara said. "You really came through. Meghan Salinger is safe and alive, back with her family. I went and visited them yesterday. They can't believe their daughter is home. I offered to cover all of the therapy Meghan will need to recover from this horrible kidnapping."

Nicky smiled. Senator Gregory was a good woman. Nicky just wished she'd been able to save her daughter too. But Amara was strong; she was looking forward, not backwards, and Nicky admired that. Sometimes she needed to do that too.

"I have to admit," Chief Franco said, looking at Nicky and Ken, "I had some doubts about pairing you two together. But Senator Gregory wanted our best field agents on the job. Clearly, that was a good call."

Nicky felt her face heat. "Agent Walker's not so bad when you get to know him."

Ken just sat in the chair with his arms crossed, saying nothing, but Nicky knew they'd come to the same mutual respect.

"One thing doesn't quite make sense to me, though," Franco said. "How'd you find the warehouse in the first place?"

Nicky thought back to Bernard Brown, to the eerie words he'd said. *"All roads lead to home."*

"It was a hunch, sir," Nicky said.

"Hell of a hunch," Franco added. "Well, either way, I'm glad you nailed it." He faced Amara. "Senator Gregory, I think there was something you wanted to ask these three."

"Yes." Amara smiled at them, clasping her hands together over her terracotta dress-suit. "As we discussed before, Meghan Salinger was only the first of several missing women in the county. It's an alarming number of them. I'd like to ask Agent Walker and Agent Lyons, with the help of Grace here, to take on the rest of the cases. A permanent position as my task force specifically dedicated to finding these missing girls."

Not long ago, Nicky would have been afraid of the commitment. Afraid that she might fail. But she'd saved Meghan. She'd won.

"I'll definitely think about it," Nicky said.

"Same," said Ken.

"Well, you can count me in!" Grace replied.

"Perfect," Amara said. "That's all I can ask. If it were up to me, every missing girl would be found. We can only focus on one at a time, but I have so much confidence in you all."

"It's an honor, Senator," Nicky said.

Amara walked over to stand in the middle of the room. "We're so lucky to have such excellent agents in our midst." She looked at Grace. "And you've certainly proven yourself to be one of the best techs around. I'm glad you're leveraging your skill to our advantage."

Grace blushed and gave Amara a nod. The senator nodded back, and then headed to the door. "Think about what I said, Agents," Amara said. "I'll be in touch soon." With that, Amara left the room.

"She's a good woman," Chief Franco said. "We should be proud to work with her."

Nicky nodded. A solemn silence filled the room. She and Ken sat there, thinking of all the women who'd gone missing. Of Meghan. Of all the lives she'd saved.

"Hey."

Nicky turned to Ken.

"For what it's worth, I think you can do this," Ken said. "You were a good leader, Lyons. Your instincts were spot on. And that's coming from someone who hates sharing the spotlight."

Nicky smiled. "Thanks, Walker."

Everyone stood up and shook hands—except for Grace, who went for a hug. Then, they all broke apart. Job well done. Much more to do. Nicky had the rest of the day off, and she considered going to sit on a patio and have a nice cold beer—but maybe that wasn't what was best for her right now.

There was someone she hadn't seen in a while, someone she'd been meaning to visit.

***

The walls of Dr. Graham's office were a deep red, with a fish tank on one wall. Nicky sat in his chair, facing her psychiatrist as he calmly spoke. The water in the tank was cloudy and green, and the fish swimming around it were silver and gold. The light from the window reflecting off of the water made the fish swim in circles. Nicky felt calm and at ease in Dr. Graham's office.

"Miss Lyons," Dr. Graham said, "I didn't expect to see you for a while."

Nicky gave him a tight smile. Dr. Graham used to have Nicky on medication for her anxiety and PTSD, but even though it made the flashbacks go away... well, Nicky didn't like that. Because the flashbacks, the memories--they were all she had left of Rosie.

"I'm just here to talk, not for any meds," Nicky said.

"I know. You know I'm your therapist too."

Dr. Graham was an older man with thinning gray hair. He always wore a suit, but his tie was loose around his neck. Nicky had been seeing him for a few years now.

"Do you think you're actually up to talking?" he asked.

"Absolutely," Nicky said. A real smile came to her face. "I'm looking forward to it."

"Well, I'm glad," Dr. Graham said. "Because it's been a while since we talked. How are you, really, Nicky?"

"Good. Getting better."

"I'm glad to hear it. You're doing well in your job?"

"I'm just making it up as I go," Nicky said. "But we just had a major win, so I'm doing okay."

"Good. Drinking less?"

"On the job? Of course," Nicky said cheekily.

Dr. Graham laughed. "You know what I mean."

Nicky sighed, going quiet for a moment. "I have a drink sometimes, but it's nothing detrimental."

"Just be careful. You know it... runs in your blood."

It struck a chord for Nicky, and she paused.

For the first time in a long time, she thought of her father.

He had never been a great man, or a particularly good father. But after Rosie had disappeared, he hit the bottle hard. Work started to suffer. He lost his job. He got fired. Then, he went on a bender and ended up in jail. He wasn't there long, but when he got out, he was even more of a monster.

Nicky hated that her father had let her down. She hated his behavior, and she hated that she had failed to save Rosie.

133

He had always blamed her. Just like she'd blamed herself.

Other times, he'd be so drunk that Nicky wondered if he'd even remembered Rosie's name. He did things that drove her mother crazy. If Nicky hadn't been there, she didn't know if her mother would have gotten through it all.

Given that her mother had been as broken as Nicky, she doubted it. One day, Nicky had gone to her mother and told her she was moving away to become an FBI agent. Her mother had hugged her, and said she was proud of her.

Nicky's father, on the other hand, was not.

"What do you think you can do, Nicky? Save Rosie? It's too late for that. Maybe you're trying to make it all better, but it never will be!"

And he was right; no amount of women saved would ever replace Rosie, but at least Nicky was doing something good with her life. Nicky hadn't seen her father in years, but as far as she knew, he was still a drunk, and still in West Virginia.

Nicky's mother had died of cancer when Nicky was twenty. Nicky always wondered if the stress of losing Rosie had contributed to it spreading so fast. But her mother had been kind and warm. Not like her father. Her sorry excuse for a dad didn't deserve her, or his family.

Snapping back to Dr. Graham's office, Nicky sighed. "I know. I pace myself. I don't drink too much."

"Good. I know you deal with a lot of guilt, Nicky." Dr. Graham paused. "That's why you're here."

"Yeah," Nicky said. "It's hard, sometimes, to not hate myself for getting away. I hate that I'm out here living while Rosie is... gone." Nicky wouldn't say 'dead' because she didn't know if Rosie was dead. A body was never found.

"I know," Dr. Graham said. "It's a hard thing, I know."

Nicky nodded. She stared at the fish tank, at the bubbling water, and shut her eyes.

The lake house came back to her again.

Plunging into the dark water...

How had it become both the place of her dreams and her nightmares?

She knew what she'd do if she ever made it there again. And she was so afraid of it, but at the same time, she needed to see it--to touch it--for closure.

"I want to be good at this," she said. "I want to be the best."

Dr. Graham smiled. "You already are, Nicky. Sometimes I forget that you're only twenty-nine. You've already been through so much."

"Not all of it bad."

He laughed. "You have that right. But I do wish you'd open up to people more."

For the first time in a long time, Nicky remembered that Matt had reached out to her online. Matt, who Nicky once considered a best friend back home, was a stranger to her now. But she still had all those memories of him.

It was true; Nicky didn't let a lot of people in, not really in. It wasn't just boyfriends--it was friends too. Nicky could talk about herself no problem, but she'd always struggled to maintain those real friendships that lasted, like the friendships she'd had with her group of friends back in high school. And Matt was one of those friends.

It was strange to think of him after all this time.

"I don't know," Nicky said. "With how complicated my life is, sometimes I think it's better to just keep people out."

Dr. Graham smiled in a grandfatherly way. Nicky knew he was about to drop some of his wisdom on her, which was nice, considering her father had never been one to give her that. Dr. Graham was a great therapist.

He was always calm and collected. Always looked like he was the one on the top of the world.

"Nicky, that's never going to work."

"What?" she asked.

"You can't keep people out forever. It's okay to need people, but that means you have to let them in at some point."

Maybe he was right. Nicky thought back to that night with Ken, when they'd confided in each other. It was weird for her to do that, especially with someone she barely knew, but at the same time, learning Ken's story had made her feel... understood.

Maybe it wouldn't be so bad to have a friend to talk to, outside of work, every now and then.

"Thanks, Dr. Graham," Nicky said. "I'll think about it."

As she walked out of his office, she couldn't help but think back to her father.

He'd always been the stereotypical angry drunk, and it was frustrating, because Nicky had always tried to save him. She'd tried to make him better. But he was never a good man. He treated her mother poorly, and after Rosie was gone, he'd treated Nicky like shit too.

Nicky's family was broken, maybe even before Rosie went missing. But Nicky owed it to Rosie to remember her as the person she'd always been: a good person.

Whenever Nicky thought of Rosie, she thought of that time at the lake house.

But they had memories before that, too.

Memories from when they were normal sisters.

When they were little--Nicky was nine and Rosie was eight--their father still had a shred of kindness in him.

He got Rosie a puppy for her birthday.

The puppy was a standard poodle. It had lots of white fur and a floppy, curly tail. It was always a little nervous, an anxious little thing. But Rosie had always been anxious too.

Nicky remembered playing with the dog with Rosie in the living room of their old home. How happy Rosie had been.

There were other happy memories too.

When Nicky was ten and Rosie was nine, they'd gotten matching pigtails.

They'd both been so excited. They'd gotten new dresses, shoes, and handbags. Then they had gone to the nail salon to get their nails painted.

They'd had so much fun that day.

Nicky remembered this all as clearly as if it had just happened yesterday. She remembered the way the little pigtails looked on her little sister.

She remembered the way Rosie was always happy.

Another time, they had decided to start up a lemonade stand. They got a stand and some old, beat-up folding tables, and they set up in the front yard.

They set the tables out in the sun, facing the road.

It was summer, so the sun hit them straight-on, and the heat from the flowers on the fence warmed the table legs.

They set up their stuff and Rosie made them some lemonade. They sold it to the neighbors and made a lot of money.

They had all the time in the world.

Nicky remembered them eating ice cream after the stand closed. The cool sweet flavor of the ice cream. The coolness that filled her mouth.

She remembered Rosie being happy.

And most of all, she reminded herself that it was okay to think of the good times. She didn't have to keep torturing herself with memories of when everything went wrong. There was so much more to Rosie and Nicky's life than those horrible three days in that cabin. So much more.

136

But remembering all of that happiness only made Nicky's resolve burn brighter.

She couldn't give up on Rosie.

Because Rosie never would have given up on her.

EPILOGUE

Nicky sat on her couch and looked out the window at Jacksonville. The sky was clear, smooth, and faintly blue. She could see the hotel and casino across the bay, lit up by the early evening sun. A gentle breeze wafted from the bay, carried on the salty air. Nicky could smell the salt in the air and feel it on her skin.

It felt good to be home.

After what Dr. Graham had said, Nicky was feeling more optimistic about the future--and about letting someone into her life. Or someone back into her life.

She opened up her laptop and went on social media, where she opened the message from Matt. Nicky hesitated. It had been so long since she'd seen him. Or anyone from home. It'd been so long since she'd seen someone who actually knew Rosie in real life.

Maybe it would be triggering for her. Matt was a reminder of her past, a reminder of her home. Jacksonville, and Florida in general, was a different world from West Virginia.

Nicky had a lot of memories of Matt. Most of them were good. She remembered how he used to be able to tease her about her goofy family and her goofy friends. He was fun. He was smart. He was funny.

He'd also helped her through the first few months after Rosie went missing. He'd tried so hard to make sure Nicky was okay. But she also had some memories that were less than pleasant.

Matt had been where she felt the most alone, and that was when she was in his arms. She'd had a hard enough time without having him be a part of the pain. They never dated, they were just close friends, but Nicky knew that Matt had always had a soft spot for her.

And now he was back for her.

The key to her heart had always been hard to find.

But maybe she could at least accept Matt's olive branch and go for coffee or something.

She messaged him back, saying:

Hey Matt--I gave your offer some more thought. Would you want to meet for coffee soon?

Thanks.

Nik.

138

Nicky stared at her screen for a bit, then looked back out the window. She turned off the computer and stretched out on the couch, staring at the ceiling. Now, all she had to do was wait for an answer, but it felt like taking that first step. She was ready to see him again-- ready to face her past again.

Nicky stood up and went into her room. In the drawer of her dresser, she dug through some papers until she found a single photo. Nicky carefully extracted it from the drawer of her dresser. It was a Polaroid taken with a small camera. It was time-stained, but the picture still held a certain charm. Nicky smiled at the photo.

It was of Rosie.

Her sister's brown hair and freckled face brought back too many memories. Some good. Some bad.

It had always killed her that Rosie's case went cold. Even with Nicky's statement, they had never been able to find the man who'd abducted them. But Nicky would never forget his face. It was ingrained into her mind.

Rosie's eyes stared back at her.

I can't quit thinking about you, Rosie. Even after all this time.

It haunted her nightmares. He'd been so fast.

Nicky's hand shook a little as she took the photo and slipped it back into its place in the drawer.

All these years, the man had felt like a ghost. Where did he come from? Nicky had no idea. He was white, she remembered that much. American accent. He was real.

So where did he go?

And if Rosie was dead, then why didn't her body ever turn up?

Nicky shook her head. She was an FBI agent. It occurred to her that she didn't have to let this keep slipping by. She could find out who the man was. She could do something about it. She could find the asshole who took her and her sister and put him in prison.

But it wouldn't be that easy. Not at all.

By now, Nicky felt like she had a lot of questions, but she hadn't been able to find the answers.

But now she knew she needed to keep going.

She gazed out the large windows of the living room and saw the skyline of Jacksonville. The sun was just peeking over the horizon, casting a long, golden shadow across the bay. The buildings were so brightly lit that they almost appeared to be on fire. The bright blue sky was a painting on the horizon, and it looked so peaceful and calm.

Rosie would love this view. Nicky wanted to have her here someday, to show her.

Nicky took a deep breath, then marched to the second bedroom, the room she'd dedicated to Rosie. It had every picture Nicky had. Every newspaper clipping. Every video and every report she'd ever done. She'd had to spend hours putting it together. She'd read so much about her sister, so many stories that told her she was dead. But she was alive. She was somewhere.

She hadn't stopped hoping, not even once.

As Nicky sat down in the middle of the room, on the soft carpet, she closed her eyes.

She had to find the man who took Rosie.

She had to make him pay.

And she would.

Rosie had been gone for a long time. Her case had been declared cold years ago. But she was looking down on Nicky from wherever she was. She was looking down on Nicky as she finally made up her mind.

Nicky wasn't going to let it go. She wasn't going to keep staring at all these photos and articles. And she wasn't going to keep calling the police station in Nelly, just to scratch a phantom itch.

No. She was going to look for Rosie. And she was going to find her.

NOW AVAILABLE!

ALL HIS
(A Nicky Lyons FBI Suspense Thriller—Book 2)

When a senator's daughter goes missing, it is a race against time as FBI Special Agent Nicky Lyons, 28, a fast-rising star in the BAU, is tasked with finding her—and with finding, per the senator's order, the top 10 abducted women most likely to still be alive. When a kidnapper abducts female twins, giving one a chance to escape while the other is killed, Nicky wonders: could this be the same killer who took her own sister more than a decade ago?

"A masterpiece of thriller and mystery."
—Books and Movie Reviews, Roberto Mattos (re Once Gone)

ALL HIS (A Nicky Lyons FBI Suspense Thriller—Book 2) is book #2 in a new series by #1 bestselling and critically acclaimed mystery and suspense author Blake Pierce.

Nicky Lyons, 28, a missing-persons specialist in in the FBI's Behavioral Analysis Unit, is an expert at tracking down abductees and bringing them home. The connection is personal: after Nicky's twin sister was abducted at 16, Nicky made stopping kidnappers her life's work.

But when Nicky is assigned to a new task force in south Florida dedicated to finding the recently missing, she soon realizes she's up against a serial killer more diabolical than she imagined. Her only hope at finding these girls is entering his mind and outwitting him at his own game.

Nicky and her new partner, both headstrong, don't see eye to eye, and the case opens decade-old wounds related to her sister's disappearance. Can Nicky keep her demons at bay in time to save the victims?

Nicky, haunted by the demons of her own missing sister, knows that time will be of the essence in bringing these girls home—if it is not already too late.

A page-turning and harrowing crime thriller featuring a brilliant and tortured FBI agent, the NICKY LYONS series is a riveting mystery, packed with non-stop action, suspense, twists and turns, revelations, and driven by a breakneck pace that will keep you flipping pages late into the night. Fans of Rachel Caine, Teresa Driscoll and Robert Dugoni are sure to fall in love.

Book #3 in the series—ALL HE SEES—is also available.

"An edge of your seat thriller in a new series that keeps you turning pages! ...So many twists, turns and red herrings... I can't wait to see what happens next."
—Reader review (Her Last Wish)

"A strong, complex story about two FBI agents trying to stop a serial killer. If you want an author to capture your attention and have you guessing, yet trying to put the pieces together, Pierce is your author!"
—Reader review (Her Last Wish)

"A typical Blake Pierce twisting, turning, roller coaster ride suspense thriller. Will have you turning the pages to the last sentence of the last chapter!!!"
—Reader review (City of Prey)

"Right from the start we have an unusual protagonist that I haven't seen done in this genre before. The action is nonstop... A very atmospheric novel that will keep you turning pages well into the wee hours."
—Reader review (City of Prey)

"Everything that I look for in a book... a great plot, interesting characters, and grabs your interest right away. The book moves along at a breakneck pace and stays that way until the end. Now on go I to book two!"
—Reader review (Girl, Alone)

Blake Pierce

Blake Pierce is the USA Today bestselling author of the RILEY PAGE mystery series, which includes seventeen books. Blake Pierce is also the author of the MACKENZIE WHITE mystery series, comprising fourteen books; of the AVERY BLACK mystery series, comprising six books; of the KERI LOCKE mystery series, comprising five books; of the MAKING OF RILEY PAIGE mystery series, comprising six books; of the KATE WISE mystery series, comprising seven books; of the CHLOE FINE psychological suspense mystery, comprising six books; of the JESSE HUNT psychological suspense thriller series, comprising twenty four books; of the AU PAIR psychological suspense thriller series, comprising three books; of the ZOE PRIME mystery series, comprising six books; of the ADELE SHARP mystery series, comprising sixteen books, of the EUROPEAN VOYAGE cozy mystery series, comprising four books; of the new LAURA FROST FBI suspense thriller, comprising nine books (and counting); of the new ELLA DARK FBI suspense thriller, comprising eleven books (and counting); of the A YEAR IN EUROPE cozy mystery series, comprising nine books, of the AVA GOLD mystery series, comprising six books (and counting); of the RACHEL GIFT mystery series, comprising eight books (and counting); of the VALERIE LAW mystery series, comprising nine books (and counting); of the PAIGE KING mystery series, comprising six books (and counting); of the MAY MOORE mystery series, comprising six books (and counting); the CORA SHIELDS mystery series, comprising three books (and counting); and the NICKY LYONS FBI suspense thriller series, comprising three books (and counting).

An avid reader and lifelong fan of the mystery and thriller genres, Blake loves to hear from you, so please feel free to visit www.blakepierceauthor.com to learn more and stay in touch.

NO ESCAPE (Book #9)

RACHEL GIFT MYSTERY SERIES
HER LAST WISH (Book #1)
HER LAST CHANCE (Book #2)
HER LAST HOPE (Book #3)
HER LAST FEAR (Book #4)
HER LAST CHOICE (Book #5)
HER LAST BREATH (Book #6)
HER LAST MISTAKE (Book #7)
HER LAST DESIRE (Book #8)

AVA GOLD MYSTERY SERIES
CITY OF PREY (Book #1)
CITY OF FEAR (Book #2)
CITY OF BONES (Book #3)
CITY OF GHOSTS (Book #4)
CITY OF DEATH (Book #5)
CITY OF VICE (Book #6)

A YEAR IN EUROPE
A MURDER IN PARIS (Book #1)
DEATH IN FLORENCE (Book #2)
VENGEANCE IN VIENNA (Book #3)
A FATALITY IN SPAIN (Book #4)

ELLA DARK FBI SUSPENSE THRILLER
GIRL, ALONE (Book #1)
GIRL, TAKEN (Book #2)
GIRL, HUNTED (Book #3)
GIRL, SILENCED (Book #4)
GIRL, VANISHED (Book 5)
GIRL ERASED (Book #6)
GIRL, FORSAKEN (Book #7)
GIRL, TRAPPED (Book #8)
GIRL, EXPENDABLE (Book #9)
GIRL, ESCAPED (Book #10)
GIRL, HIS (Book #11)

LAURA FROST FBI SUSPENSE THRILLER

ALREADY GONE (Book #1)
ALREADY SEEN (Book #2)
ALREADY TRAPPED (Book #3)
ALREADY MISSING (Book #4)
ALREADY DEAD (Book #5)
ALREADY TAKEN (Book #6)
ALREADY CHOSEN (Book #7)
ALREADY LOST (Book #8)
ALREADY HIS (Book #9)

EUROPEAN VOYAGE COZY MYSTERY SERIES
MURDER (AND BAKLAVA) (Book #1)
DEATH (AND APPLE STRUDEL) (Book #2)
CRIME (AND LAGER) (Book #3)
MISFORTUNE (AND GOUDA) (Book #4)
CALAMITY (AND A DANISH) (Book #5)
MAYHEM (AND HERRING) (Book #6)

ADELE SHARP MYSTERY SERIES
LEFT TO DIE (Book #1)
LEFT TO RUN (Book #2)
LEFT TO HIDE (Book #3)
LEFT TO KILL (Book #4)
LEFT TO MURDER (Book #5)
LEFT TO ENVY (Book #6)
LEFT TO LAPSE (Book #7)
LEFT TO VANISH (Book #8)
LEFT TO HUNT (Book #9)
LEFT TO FEAR (Book #10)
LEFT TO PREY (Book #11)
LEFT TO LURE (Book #12)
LEFT TO CRAVE (Book #13)
LEFT TO LOATHE (Book #14)
LEFT TO HARM (Book #15)
LEFT TO RUIN (Book #16)

THE AU PAIR SERIES
ALMOST GONE (Book#1)
ALMOST LOST (Book #2)
ALMOST DEAD (Book #3)

SILENT NEIGHBOR (Book #4)
HOMECOMING (Book #5)
TINTED WINDOWS (Book #6)

KATE WISE MYSTERY SERIES
IF SHE KNEW (Book #1)
IF SHE SAW (Book #2)
IF SHE RAN (Book #3)
IF SHE HID (Book #4)
IF SHE FLED (Book #5)
IF SHE FEARED (Book #6)
IF SHE HEARD (Book #7)

THE MAKING OF RILEY PAIGE SERIES
WATCHING (Book #1)
WAITING (Book #2)
LURING (Book #3)
TAKING (Book #4)
STALKING (Book #5)
KILLING (Book #6)

RILEY PAIGE MYSTERY SERIES
ONCE GONE (Book #1)
ONCE TAKEN (Book #2)
ONCE CRAVED (Book #3)
ONCE LURED (Book #4)
ONCE HUNTED (Book #5)
ONCE PINED (Book #6)
ONCE FORSAKEN (Book #7)
ONCE COLD (Book #8)
ONCE STALKED (Book #9)
ONCE LOST (Book #10)
ONCE BURIED (Book #11)
ONCE BOUND (Book #12)
ONCE TRAPPED (Book #13)
ONCE DORMANT (Book #14)
ONCE SHUNNED (Book #15)
ONCE MISSED (Book #16)
ONCE CHOSEN (Book #17)

MACKENZIE WHITE MYSTERY SERIES
BEFORE HE KILLS (Book #1)
BEFORE HE SEES (Book #2)
BEFORE HE COVETS (Book #3)
BEFORE HE TAKES (Book #4)
BEFORE HE NEEDS (Book #5)
BEFORE HE FEELS (Book #6)
BEFORE HE SINS (Book #7)
BEFORE HE HUNTS (Book #8)
BEFORE HE PREYS (Book #9)
BEFORE HE LONGS (Book #10)
BEFORE HE LAPSES (Book #11)
BEFORE HE ENVIES (Book #12)
BEFORE HE STALKS (Book #13)
BEFORE HE HARMS (Book #14)

AVERY BLACK MYSTERY SERIES
CAUSE TO KILL (Book #1)
CAUSE TO RUN (Book #2)
CAUSE TO HIDE (Book #3)
CAUSE TO FEAR (Book #4)
CAUSE TO SAVE (Book #5)
CAUSE TO DREAD (Book #6)

KERI LOCKE MYSTERY SERIES
A TRACE OF DEATH (Book #1)
A TRACE OF MURDER (Book #2)
A TRACE OF VICE (Book #3)
A TRACE OF CRIME (Book #4)
A TRACE OF HOPE (Book #5)

Made in the USA
Columbia, SC
16 June 2024

37219105R00087